This book belongs to:

_____

(Use the chart of hieroglyphs below to spell out your name.)

Meroitic Hieroglyphs

A	B	C	D	E
F	G	H	I	J
K	L	M	N	O
P	Q	R	S	T
U	V	W	X	Y	Z

PRAISE FOR

AZ and the LOST

"AZ and the Lost City of Ophir is the best kids' adventure book you'll read anywhere, anytime. I know this because the level of jealousy I have for the author Andrew Zimmern can be detected from space. That's how good this book is. I know this is not a healthy way to evaluate the quality of things in one's life but the result is the same. AZ is OUTSTANDING."

Joel McHale, *actor, comedian, tall sock wearer*

"To be ten again! I wish this book was around when I was kid. Andrew Zimmern extracted all the travels and flavors from his real life and embedded them onto the pages of this wonderful story. A true gift."

Bobby Flay, *chef and host of multiple shows on Food Network and Cooking Channel*

"My friend Andrew is probably the most interesting man in the world. He looks at the world with childlike wonder and a completely open mind. Not only does his curiosity lead him all around the world to learn about cultures, he also is an amazing storyteller with the power to reach everyone—women, men, and children. I cannot wait to see where little AZ goes next!"

José Andrés, *chef/owner, ThinkFoodGroup & minibar by José Andrés*

CITY OF OPHIR

"AZ and the Lost City of Ophir is fun, thrilling, and a breeze to read. The characters are relatable and whimsical, making it a solid page-turner. Even I couldn't put it down—my kids are going to love this!"

Michael Solomonov, co-owner and chef of Zahav

"This book is pure Zimmern—it brings a strange and beautiful world into focus and offers equal parts adventure, fun, and information. I'd follow Andrew and H.E. McElhatton anywhere, especially into a lost city with terrifying feasts! It's exactly the type of book I devoured as a nine-year-old, and it's perfect for anyone today who loves mystery, mischief, and suspense."

Dana Cowin, host of Speaking Broadly and longtime former editor-in-chief of Food & Wine magazine

"Andrew Zimmern's work has always been about connection, love, and exploration of worlds amazing and new. AZ and the Lost City of Ophir gives you all that. Zimmern is an exceptional storyteller who leads from his big open heart and the deep desire to understand and share the mysteries of humanity. What a joy to read this fine book."

Brian Koppelman, co-creator and showrunner of Billions and co-writer of Rounders and Ocean's Thirteen

THE **ALLIANCE** OF
WORLD EXPLORERS

presents

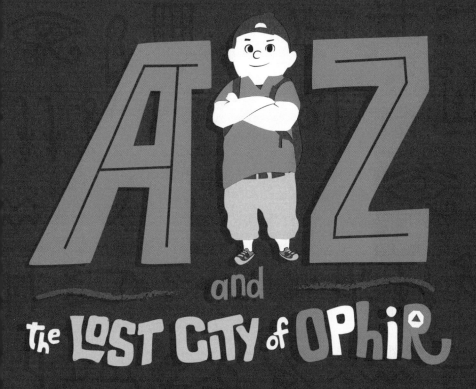

A to Z

and

the LOST CITY of OPHiR

A to Z

and

the LOST CITY of OPHIR

written by

ANDREW ZIMMERN

&

H. E. MCELHATTON

illustrated by

LISA TROUTMAN

— Beaver's Pond Press —
Edina, MN

Written by Andrew Zimmern and H. E. McElhatton
Edited by Angela Wiechmann and Julia Heffelfinger
Illustrated by Lisa Troutman
Original character designs by Gasket Studios Ltd
Managing editor: Hanna Kjeldbjerg

ISBN 13: 978-1-64343-986-0
Library of Congress Catalog Number: 2018909982
Printed in Canada
Second Printing: 2019
23 22 21 20 19   6 5 4 3 2

Book design and typesetting by Kevin Cannon.

Beaver's Pond Press
7108 Ohms Lane
Edina, MN 55439–2129
(952) 829-8818
www.BeaversPondPress.com

BEAVER'S
POND
PRESS

To order, visit www.ItascaBooks.com
or call (800)-901-3480. Reseller discounts available.

For media inquiries, please call or email Justin Loeber, Mouth : Digital + Public Relations, 212-260-7576; justin.loeber@mouthdigitalpr.com.

Acknowledgments

*Andrew Zimmern and H. E. McElhatton
would like to thank all the strange creatures
who helped them create this book:*

The dastardly duo of John Larson and Tom Wiese
Secret weapon Stephanie Unterberger and the
    Wiese Law Firm
The wonderfully weird Pirner family
The sickly smart Siegert family
Evil geniuses Ruby and Daisy Barone
Über Overlords John and Jane McKean
Andapanda Stink and Devil-Baby David
Tiny Terrible Tim
El Barto
Weird Cousin Wes
Creepy Colin
Jumpin' Jack Judeman
Wonderful Walter
Hanna and the amazing Beaver's Pond Press team
Illustrious illustrator Lisa Troutman
Julia Heffelfinger
Kevin Cannon
Gasket Studios Ltd
Rebecca & The Brookettes
Josh and the team at WME
Noah Zimmern for his inspiration
Rishia Zimmern, the Queen of Patience and
    Tolerance

Table of Contents

1 A SPECTACULAR DISASTER ——— 1

2 ODD UNCLE ARTHUR ——— 12

3 THE ALLIANCE ——— 27

4 THE ACCIDENTAL EXPLORERS ——— 51

5 THE BLACK PYRAMID ——— 74

6 THE LOST CITY OF SECRETS ——— 86

7 TRIED, TRUE, AND TESTED ——— 105

8 THE EYE OF HORUS ——— 114

9 THE RUBY TABLET ——— 123

10 DOOMED AND ENTOMBED ——— 136

11 THE DEAD AWAKEN ——— 153

12 THE GREAT GROSS-OFF ——— 166

13 THE NEW WORLD EXPLORERS ——— 184

TOP SECRET!!! ——— 199

ABOUT THE AUTHORS ——— 220

THIS BOOK IS DEDICATED
to all the children of the world.
Brave, adventurous, smart,
and funny, our children
are our future.

And especially to my brave son,
Noah, for whom the world is an
endless playground
of possibility.

-AZ

A SPECTACULAR DISASTER

I t's a disaster. A gloppy, sloppy, gooey, gorilla-size disaster. It's completely Dad's fault—he knows better than to walk into my room without knocking. Unless he knocks, how can I know to shut off all the anti-intruder alarms and countertactical weaponry before he walks through the door?

Plus, he's ruined my experiment! I had finally perfected my recipe for Master Blaster Exploding Foam and was working on it before he barged in. My desk was covered with bottles and beakers and various dangerous chemicals I'd ordered online. (It was hard enough getting that package past my parents.) I was just pouring the catalyst—yeast and water in a small yellow bottle—into a large green bottle filled with dish soap, industrial-strength hydrogen peroxide, and a few drops of green dye.

CHAPTER ONE

That's when Dad charged into my room! He set off all the alarms, nearly giving me a heart attack. The yellow bottle dropped out of my hand and splashed into the green bottle. There was a sizzling sound and then . . .

BOOM!

A massive volcano of green foam exploded all over the room. Now my room is like a swimming pool filled to the top with foam. Dad got blasted right in the face and is completely covered, slipping on the wet floor.

"WHOA-OH-OH!" he shouts as he goes crashing down to the floor.

I can't see him now, but I can hear him groan as the still-expanding puffy green mountain of Master Blaster Exploding Foam closes over him.

"Dad?" I cough, wiping green foam from my safety goggles. "You OK?"

Dad lies there groaning. His arm rises up out of the foam. He's clutching a damp mint-green index card in his hand. My stomach does a queasy flip.

"Any idea what this is?" he asks.

"I have no idea," I say, even though I know *exactly* what it is.

"It's your report card," he says. He spits out a puff of foam. "Any idea how you did this semester?"

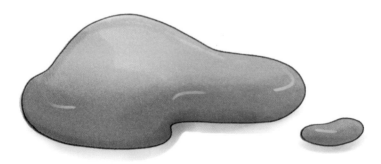

CHAPTER ONE

I shake my head, even though I know *exactly* how I did. I did badly. *Very badly.*

"AZ, you promised to get your grades up by the end of the year, remember?"

"Actually, I think I said I'd *try* to get my grades up."

"No, you *promised*. Seriously, AZ—you're twelve years old now and going into the seventh grade. You're not a little kid anymore. Your grades matter. That's why we all agreed you had to get your grades up by the end of the year if you wanted to go on the—"

"Hey, Dad!" I cut him off and lean forward, putting my hand to my ear. "Did Mom just call us for dinner?"

"I didn't hear anything."

"I think she did. I think your ears might have foam in them."

Suddenly, I hear Mom yell from downstairs, "Hey, guys! Dinner is ready!"

Saved!

"Sorry, Dad. Gotta go! Mom hates it when I'm late to the dinner table."

"AZ, we're not finished talking about this!"

I get up and sprint for the door, jumping over the foamy lump that is my dad as I hustle downstairs.

Mom is bent over the stove. "Have you washed your hands?" she asks.

"Yep! Sure did!"

As soon as she's not looking, I stick my hands into the goldfish bowl on the counter. I swish them around with our two orange goldfish, Princess McNugget and Free Gilly. They don't mind when I use their bowl as a hand-washing station. They like the excitement.

Mom stands up as I finish drying my hands on my cargo

shorts—or as I call them, my adventure pants. I wear them every day, in case of an unexpected adventure. I made them myself. They're cutoff cargo pants with extra pockets stitched on. The pockets are filled with gear every great explorer needs: maps, matches, flashlights, field journals, snacks (of both the hot and cold variety), and an assortment of my secret concoctions and inventions.

For now, though, my next adventure is dinner.

"So, what's for dinner, Mom?"

"Squid and linguine."

"Yes!"

I love squid and linguine. I love all food, really, but especially food other people think is weird. My parents are archaeologists, and we've traveled all over the world visiting dig sites, conferences, and exhibitions. Throughout our travels, I acquired what they call a "complex palate." That's fancy-talk for an "iron gut."

I can eat anything, no matter how strange, stinky, spoiled, slimy, slithery, sloppy, bloody, muddy, gritty, grimy, grungy, or *gross*. I've eaten live ants, squashed worms, and grasshoppers dipped in gravy (a personal favorite).

Kids at my school in Minneapolis pay good money to watch me eat gross things. Tommy paid me ten bucks to eat three dead cockroaches he collected from behind the bleachers in the school gym. Alex bet me five bucks to finish off a rancid meat loaf we found in the cafeteria's dumpster. And Martha reluctantly gave me seven bucks after I ate a whole jalapeño pepper— in one bite.

CHAPTER ONE

Sure, it's gross or uncomfortable sometimes, but I've always made a very nice living, thanks to my freakish ability. The money pads my allowance every week, which is good. I need the extra cash because AZ, the world's greatest explorer, is about to embark on his most spectacular adventure yet.

This summer, I'm going to do something on my BIG (Before I'm Grown-up) List, which I keep in my adventure journal. Our whole family is going on the dig together. We're even taking my little brother, Scottie, who's never been on a dig before. He's a total pain, though. All he does is wobble around crashing into things, shrieking like a teakettle! Anyways, because the dig will go the entire summer, my parents got special permission to bring us kids along with them. It's going to be so freaking *cool*!

The dig is in the Siberian tundra in Russia. We'll spend all summer unearthing . . . wait for it . . . an actual, real-life woolly mammoth! An eight-ton prehistoric woolly mammoth that died over ten thousand years ago and is buried deep inside a glacier. Dad says being encased in a cold, oxygen-free atmosphere has kept the mammoth perfectly preserved all these centuries. We might even be able to look inside the woolly mammoth's stomach and see what he ate for his last supper!

I'm so excited. This is the big time. This is officially the beginning. My career as the world's greatest explorer has begun!

Dad has the mint-green index card in his hand as he limps into the kitchen and sits down. Mom brings over a steaming bowl and sets it down in the middle of the table. I catch my dad's stern expression through the curling ribbons of steam rising from the bowl of linguine. He clears his throat and stares at me.

My BIG
Adventure List

What?	Where?	Notes?
* Live Underwater	The Caribbean Ocean	* Design airtight gerbil ball & roll on ocean floor
* Discover an Egyptian Tomb	Egyptian Desert	* Make sure it's a tomb filled with GOLD
* Colonize the Moon	Outer Space	* Pitstop at the International Space Station
* Discover & Own An Uninhabited Island	???	* Island name: Badboylandia Population: ME! Motto: Weird is good
* See the Library of Ashurbanipal	Somewhere in Iraq	* Over 22000 cuneiform clay tablets were found there & supposedly contain the secret to eternal life
* Discover a lost Incan city with LOTS of Incan gold	Peru	* Learn how to appease Incan gods before you awaken them...
* See Galapagos Islands	West Ecuador	* Befriend a Komodo dragon & train it to do tricks
* Go on a safari in Africa	Kenya	* Find a Maasai warrior tribe that will adopt me & teach me how to throw spear/jump high!

CHAPTER ONE

"AZ, we still need to talk about your report card."

"Hey, Mom!" I grin at her, trying to change the subject. "That looks great!"

Mom ladles squid and linguine into each of our bowls and gives Scottie a small dish of plain linguine with butter. Scottie is a food moron. Who doesn't like squid? I'm digging into my bowl, slurping up a piece of squid and letting it hang out of my mouth like a wriggling arm.

Dad places the ominous mint-green index card in the middle of the table. Mom shifts uncomfortably in her chair.

"I thought we'd wait until after dinner, Steven," she says.

"Laura dear, it's time."

Scottie lets out a loud screech and throws his dish onto the floor. Mom calmly gets another dish of linguine for him, which he stares at.

I do not like how this conversation is going. There's something strange in my parents' voices. Dad picks up the mint-green report card and reads it.

"You failed math," he points out. "And science. And somehow you failed both PE and speech? I didn't know a person *could* fail speech. You speak, don't you?"

I set my fork down. "I told you—my math teacher is crazy, and my science teacher mutters and no one can hear him. And Mr. Kaminski, my gym teacher, hates me. He would fail me even if I swam faster than a shark—an actual living shark! He's mean. When we go swimming, he locks the kickboards in a supply closet so we can't play Smack the Quack."

Dad grunts. "Thirty-five middle school kids in a swimming pool? I'd lock myself in a supply closet."

Mom sighs. "It's your math and science classes we're worried about. Do you remember that you agreed to get your grades up?"

My heart beats faster. This conversation is not good. Not good at all. I go for pity.

"I can't help it!" I wail. "I'm just stupid! You can't be mad at a stupid person for being stupid!"

It's Dad's turn to sigh. "Every person at this table knows you're not stupid, AZ. Anyone who can figure out how much chocolate pudding mix it takes to fill our washing machine is not stupid."

"I'll do better next year! I promise!"

Dad shakes his head sadly. "I'm sorry, son, but you can't come on the dig with us."

"What?" My mouth drops open.

"I said you can't come on the dig. You'll have to stay behind and go to summer school."

I nearly choke. "Summer school? Are you serious?"

Mom puts her hand on my arm. "Honey, if you don't make up for the classes you failed, you'll have to repeat them, and you might be held back next year. That's more important than anything else."

"Mom, I'll do better next year! I will! I promise!"

"That's what you promised last year."

"But I mean it this time!"

Dad interjects, "I'm sorry, AZ. Our minds are made up."

I look at my mom and dad. Are they serious? Is this a bluff? Most importantly, can I get out of it? I try a full-frontal attack first.

"Fine. Who cares if I failed math?" I protest. "Who needs stupid math? I want to be the world's greatest explorer, not some stupid mathematician!"

"And *that*, son, is why you need summer school."

"You can't do this!" I say. "Who cares about math?"

"AZ, your mother and I care about math! We *are*

archaeologists, remember? How do you think they built those pyramids in the first place? Wishful thinking? Or did a little math come in handy? Huh, buddy?"

"Dad, please. I don't want to *build* a pyramid. I want to *discover* one! With a mountain of rubies inside and an army of undead mummies and a real, live sphinx!"

Dad squints at me hard, as he does when he's getting a bad headache. "How exactly do you plan on *cataloging all* those undead mummies?" he asks me. "With an advanced computer system or with a set of crayons?"

"Dad, come on," I say. "They have *computer techs* for cataloging all that boring junk. But I'll be the guy who escapes the evil curse and unlocks the hidden tomb filled with treasure!"

Dad closes his eyes and pinches the bridge of his nose with his forefinger and thumb. "So, let's see. You're three hundred miles out to sea, searching for shipwrecks a mile underwater on the ocean floor. Are you going to mathematically calibrate your sonar equipment or just sing it a little song?"

"What kind of song?" I tease.

"No!" Dad explodes. "No, there's no song!"

Mom cuts in. "Honey, what your father means is that it's important to know what you're doing and have all the tools available to you, especially math. A true archaeologist cares more about protecting treasures than about finding them. We're the only thing keeping all those priceless artifacts from being lost forever. A relic is safe when it's buried; the true danger is above ground. We're up against time, geography, geology, and greed. We need all the skills we can get. Excavation, cleaning, caring, preservation—science helps us save things. To be a good archaeologist, you need science and math as well as sound instincts."

"Tell him he also needs an actual degree in archaeology!"

Dad barks at Mom. "But at this rate, he won't even get into high school!"

"Mom!" I plead as tears well up in my eyes. "*Please* let me come on the dig!"

"I'm sorry, honey." Mom shakes her head. "Your father's right. We've already made up our minds. You're staying with Uncle Arthur and going to summer school."

My jaw drops. "*Uncle Arthur?*"

"Luckily, he's agreed to watch you while we're away."

I shake my head in disbelief. I can't believe they're making me spend the entire summer with my dad's older brother, Arthur. I call him Odd Uncle Arthur because, well, he's *odd*.

"It's already arranged," Mom explains. "He's picking you up the same morning we leave for the dig."

"Are you serious?"

They're serious.

I sit back, staring at them. Who *are* these horrible monsters who've taken the place of my parents? Who are these tyrant overlords ruining everything?

But it's official. My sentence is set in stone. My spectacular summer has become a spectacular disaster.

ODD UNCLE ARTHUR

My parents are leaving without me. The awful day has finally arrived. While they're finishing up their last-minute packing, I'm sitting on the front steps waiting for *Odd* Uncle Arthur.

I don't know him well because he works all the time. Doing what, I have no idea, but I know it's boring because he's boring. He's about the most boring person I've ever met. What will we talk about for three months? Probably nothing.

Luckily, I packed everything a kid might need to entertain himself for an entire summer. I've got my duffel bag, and I'm wearing my fully-stocked adventure pants, which are a *little* tight since I've gained some weight. Again. Mom warned me to be careful, because there's no more room for her to move the button over. I also have my shiny bright-yellow backpack, which is ultra-tough and completely waterproof. It's guaranteed to survive in any climate and keep whatever junk I put inside it safe and sound.

I carry everything in there, from my silver binoculars and field journals to my bug jars and portable science experiments. And don't forget my Fourth of July sparklers and emergency flares—you know, just in case.

My dad warns me that it's dangerous to carry so many chemicals and equipment together. He says someday my backpack will blow me to molecular bits. But I keep explaining that I always pack everything just the right way. Nothing dangerous comes in contact with anything explosive and vice versa. Besides, I need everything I have in there. It's the only way I'll make it through the summer and have any fun whatsoever.

It's also the only way I'll eat well. I carry snacks wherever I go. And since Uncle Arthur probably only eats boring food every boring day, I brought extra spices and condiments as well. Nothing fixes boring food quicker than Thai chili paste and fish sauce.

The screen door slams behind me. Dad carries out another set of suitcases to the long line of suitcases already lined up on the porch.

"Why the long face, son?" he asks.

I roll my eyes. "Gee, I don't know. Maybe because you guys are going on one of the coolest adventures of all time and I'm facing the worst summer ever?"

He sighs. "You'll be fine."

"No, I will *not* be fine. I will die, Dad. I will die of complete and total boredom."

"It's possible," he muses. "But you never know when your next adventure will happen."

"Well, it *won't* be at Uncle Arthur's house," I pout. "I know that much for sure."

Dad frowns at me. "Don't worry about it. Summer school will keep you plenty busy."

"Great," I tell him. "Sounds *super.*"

"Hey, Scottie!" Dad smiles as he turns to look at the door.

I look over my shoulder to see Scottie's dorky face all smooshed against the screen.

"Come say good-bye to your big brother!"

Dad opens the door, and Scottie comes tumbling out, all sticky hands and drooling. Dad grabs more suitcases from the front hall and carries them out.

I snarl at my obnoxious little brother as he wobbles toward my backpack. "Don't touch that!" I snap at him. "You'll get it all sticky!"

"Scottie's helping," Dad says as he beams.

"Scottie's *drooling.* C'mon, Dad. Please! I've really learned my lesson. I *have*. Can I *please-please-please* go with you on your expedition?"

He frowns at me. "Sorry, buddy. Maybe next year you'll take your grades more seriously."

"But why does Scottie get to go? It's not fair that you're taking him and not me!"

Upon hearing his name, Scottie claps his hands and smiles at me. I stick my tongue out at him, but that makes him laugh and clap even louder.

"You might be older," Dad says, "but Scottie's grades are way better. He got a gold star at day care. Didn't you, buddy?"

"What gets you a gold star at day care? Not peeing your pants? Eating crayons?"

Dad looks over as a long black limousine pulls into our driveway and honks loudly. A tinted rear window rolls down. To my surprise, Uncle Arthur leans out.

"We're here!" he shouts. "Is the boy ready?"

"Hey there, Arty!" my dad says with a smile. "Say hi, Scottie!"

Uncle Arthur makes a face. "Good God—I'm not taking that baby for the summer, am I?"

Dad laughs. "No, just AZ. Stand up, son. Wave to your uncle!"

I stand up. Uncle Arthur frowns at me as if I'm only slightly less disappointing.

"Very well," he says. "Let's go. We're late as it is."

I look at my dad. "Late for what?"

Dad shrugs. Then Mom comes banging out through the screen door. She waves at Uncle Arthur, then shoves an oily-bottomed paper bag at me.

"Here, I packed some treats for you."

"Thanks, Mom."

"Now you remember to behave." She wipes away a tear. "And . . . and . . . we'll see you in September." She starts to sniffle and quickly wipes another tear away.

I hug her good-bye, and Dad makes me promise for the millionth time that I'll be good and I'll behave and I won't use superglue even once while they're gone.

"Yes, Dad. OK! You told me already!"

Uncle Arthur's car starts honking again. Mom and Dad quickly hug and kiss me good-bye, while Scottie leans in and smears my cheek with something sticky. I hurry down the driveway. Before getting in the limo, I look back and wave at them one final time, thinking, *Bye! You'll be sorry you left me behind when you find me dead from boredom!*

Suddenly, I'm sitting in the back seat of a stretch limo with Uncle Arthur.

"Well, *that* took long enough," he snorts. "Hey, Singh?" he calls to his driver.

The driver nods. He's a dark-eyed man with a large red turban wrapped around his head.

"That's Singh," Uncle Arthur says to me. "He's one of the best drivers in the world. He's broken all the known speed records in racing at one time or another. Haven't you, Singh?"

Singh nods slightly in the rearview mirror.

I look over at my uncle, still
a bit in shock. A limo with a

private driver? Odd Uncle Arthur, indeed!

"So, Uncle Arthur, where exactly are we going?"

"It's not *where*, dear boy. It's *what*."

"OK, to what are we going?"

"We are going to an exhibition. One of the most exciting exhibitions of all time."

We merge onto the highway and speed east. Before long, I start seeing signs for the airport.

"Um, Uncle Arthur? Where is this exhibition?"

"London, of course. All the best exhibitions are at the British Museum." He regards me casually. "You have your passport, of course?"

"Well, actually, I do have my passport. But . . . but . . . I can't—"

CHAPTER TWO

"Singh could have smuggled you through customs, of course," Uncle Arthur interrupts. "He's a world-renowned smuggler. But it would be such a bother to lower you into an empty fuel tank."

"What?"

"Once Singh smuggled the princess of Denmark out of a ghastly situation at a Swedish film festival. He was knighted and given a Medal of Honor for bravery in the field."

I decide not to ask any more questions.

Twenty minutes later, we pull into the Minneapolis–Saint Paul International Airport, then we turn down a long sloping road marked "Private Aircraft Only."

I look out the window. "Um, Uncle Arthur? Did you tell my mom and dad we'd be flying to London?"

"No. Why would I?"

"I'm supposed to start summer school on Monday."

"What on earth is summer school?"

"It's like regular school, but it's during the summer." I reach into my VIP (very important papers) pocket in my adventure pants and take out my crumpled class schedule.

Uncle Arthur snorts at it. "If your parents were so concerned with micromanaging you, then they ought to have stayed home."

"Well, the teachers at summer school will be expecting me. I'm already enrolled."

"Nonsense," he says. "That's barbaric."

"I agree completely," I say quickly, "but I'm still supposed to show up Monday morning. And if I don't, my parents will kill me. They actually said they would kill me."

"Don't be silly," he says. "Singh! Get my nephew's school on the phone!"

Four seconds later, we hear a phone ring and a silver

telephone rises automatically from the armrest between us. Uncle Arthur picks up the silver receiver and clears his throat.

"Good day," he says. "To whom am I speaking? Ms. Sorenson, I'm calling to inform you that my nephew, AZ, is unable to attend summer school. *Reason for cancellation?* I see. Well, after careful examination, I've determined that my nephew would learn more from a cage of unsupervised orangutans than from the dank cinder-block oubliette you call summer school. Good day."

He returns the receiver, and the telephone disappears again.

"Uncle Arthur, what does *oubliette* mean?"

"Dungeon." He leans over to look out the window as we pull into an airplane hangar. "Ah! Here we are! And not a moment too soon."

"But my parents—"

"Heavens," he says, exasperated. "Do you *want* to go to summer school? To that joyless warehouse they call an institution of learning? I thought you'd enjoy an exhibit on ancient Egypt a bit more. Nevertheless, you may stay. It's your decision, naturally."

Singh drives the limo alongside a sleek silver jet.

"Uncle Arthur," I whisper. "Is this *your* plane?"

He smiles and nods. "Her name is *Invictrix*. It's a Latin hybrid: 'She who soars and conquers.'"

I stare at the gleaming machine as we get out of the limo. The tail wing is stamped with a large official-looking seal that reads:

ALLIANCE OF WORLD EXPLORERS
SEMPER EXPLORO

Beneath the seal is a phrase I can't make out. I squint. "What's *Semper . . . Semper explo—*"

"*Semper exploro!*" Uncle Arthur shouts at me, grinning. "That's our motto. It means 'Always explore.'"

I look over at him. "What do you mean? Whose motto?"

"The Alliance, of course. The Alliance of World Explorers."

I wrinkle my brow, confused. "Dad told me you worked at some insurance company or something!"

"Yes, he did. That's because I told him I worked at an insurance company."

"Why?"

Uncle Arthur raises his eyebrow at me. "Do you want *your* little brother knowing everything *you* do?"

"No. No way." Visions of sticky hands flood my brain.

"Then you understand."

"But—"

"AZ, can you keep a secret?"

I nod silently.

"Good, because you'll hear quite a lot of them," he says. "Now, let's go."

He turns and heads for the jet. I scamper after him, lugging my duffel bag and bright-yellow backpack with me. We hurry down a long red carpet that leads from the car to the plane. Singh suddenly bounds past us, wearing a neatly ironed khaki jumpsuit, aviator goggles, and a jaunty white scarf. He's carrying a silver clipboard with a flight manifest.

I look up at Uncle Arthur. "So, Singh is also your pilot?"

"Naturally! He's one of the most decorated pilots in the world. He can fly anything. He's test-flown every top-secret aircraft at NASA."

We board the silver *Invictrix*, ducking down through the small oval door, and take our seats up front. The chairs are big, they swivel all the way around, and they're upholstered in soft white leather.

As we buckle up, I watch Singh in the cockpit. He puts on a pair of headphones, checks the instrument panel, and flips buttons and switches. I hear the engines roar up and feel a deep rumbling.

CHAPTER TWO

All of a sudden, we're out of the hangar and taxiing down the runway. We pick up speed, faster and faster, until the front wheels lift off the ground and we're up, up, and accelerating into the sky.

"Would you like something to drink?" Uncle Arthur asks when we're airborne.

I nod.

He presses a button on his armrest and speaks into it. He orders two banana smoothies, then sits back.

I'm excited, thinking a robot is about to burst out of the wall and serve us. But then Singh gets up from the cockpit and dashes past us.

"Where's he going?" I ask, more than a little nervous. "Who's flying the plane?"

"The computer's flying the plane," Uncle Arthur explains. "It's on autopilot."

I hear the clinking of glass and the whirring of a blender. Then Singh comes back with a silver tray that holds three creamy, delicious-looking banana smoothies.

"Singh is also my chef," says Uncle Arthur as he takes a smoothie and hands one to me. "He's one of the best chefs in the world. He's won all the prestigious awards. Thank you, Singh."

Singh sips his own smoothie, then returns to the cockpit.

I sip my smoothie. It tastes even more delicious that it looks. "Is that nutmeg?" I ask.

"Cardamom," says Uncle Arthur, "with a hint of cinnamon."

"It's so good!"

"I told you he was excellent."

Once we finish our smoothies, Uncle Arthur turns to me. "All right, then," he says. "First, before I tell you anything, you must take an oath of silence."

"Um, OK . . ."

"What I'm about to tell you can never be repeated, understand? It could cost lives."

Lives? All I can do is gulp. "Oh. That sounds . . . Yeah, OK. Got it."

He looks down at me seriously. "Do you swear to keep the secret, AZ?"

"Yes. Absolutely."

"Good. The Alliance of World Explorers—or the Alliance or the AWE for short—is an official organization for expert adventurers and explorers. Together, we work to solve all the great unsolved mysteries. We have pledged to find and protect every buried treasure and priceless artifact that remains unfound. We search endlessly, from the top of every mountain to the bottom of every deep blue sea. We're in a dangerous race to rescue every endangered artifact there is, before the smugglers and tomb raiders do."

"Wow. That is—so—freaking—*cool!*" I practically shout. "Can I join?"

"You?" He chortles. "The Alliance is for experts only. Not any bloke in a safari helmet can join. You have to be invited, and only the *very best* explorers in the world get invited. We're handpicked from all over the world. Once you're a member, it's for life. Look here."

He takes off his pinkie ring, which I hadn't noticed before, and hands it over. I run my fingers along its octagonal shape. I study the official AWE seal stamped on it, lightly tracing over the small diamond pyramid embedded at the center.

"All members of the Alliance wear a ring like this one," Uncle Arthur says.

Right then, I decide I will make it my life's mission to get a gold ring of my own.

"It looks good on you," Uncle Arthur says when I wedge the ring on my thumb. "Why don't you wear it a little while longer?"

"Really?"

He winks. "Just don't tell anyone at the Alliance I let you wear it, OK?"

I smile and nod, holding the brilliant golden ring up to my reading light. I must say, it *does* look excellent on my finger.

"So, what is this important exhibition we're going to?" I ask.

"Have you ever heard of King Solomon's mines?"

I haven't.

As Uncle Arthur explains, King Solomon lived back in ancient Egypt. He was rich. Stupid rich. He had a whole palace made of solid gold and mountains of rubies and diamonds piled almost to the ceiling. The Bible says King Solomon bought many of his vast treasures at a city called Ophir.

"O-what?" I ask.

"Oh-FEAR," Uncle Arthur repeats.

"What's that?"

"Only one of the greatest lost cities still undiscovered in the world!"

He goes on to tell me that to this day, nobody knows where Ophir is. Its location is a complete mystery, even though it was at one time the richest city in the world. Kings and queens from all over went there to buy their jewels and magnificent treasures. King Solomon went three times a year, loading gold, silver, and diamonds onto his ships until they were brimming.

"So, Ophir was like . . . an ancient luxury mall?" I ask.

"You could say that."

He explains that you could get anything there: exotic items, fine wines, rich foods, coveted spices, exquisite perfumes, refined wigs, rare jewels, carved ivory, silver coffins, intricate lapis lazuli gemstones, pet peacocks, trained apes, albino elephants, and, of course, gold. Gold was Ophir's signature sale item, the thing they did best. Ophirian gold was said to be the purest, most beautiful, and most coveted in the world. Buyers came from around the globe for it. And no matter how much they wanted, Ophir never ran out and never ran low. It was said they had enough gold inside those city walls to fill every ocean in the world. How the Ophirians actually got this gold and where they stored it was—and still is—a complete mystery.

I think about what I could do with all that gold. I could build a gold skyscraper or a solid-gold amusement park with the roller coasters all made of shining precious metal. I'd have enough money to buy a rocket ship launching pad *and* build my own fleet of animatronic dinosaurs so I could watch them battle.

Continuing on, Uncle Arthur tells me that many great explorers have searched for the legendary city of Ophir. David Livingstone thought Ophir was in India. Augustus Caesar thought it was in Portugal. Napoleon decided on Malacca. In the 1500s, a Spanish captain was so sure he'd discovered King Solomon's secret source of gold on an archipelago in the Pacific Ocean that he named it the Solomon Islands.

All these great explorers had searched for the real Ophir, but they'd all failed. No one had found so much as a single piece of pottery bearing the city's name.

"That's why this exhibition is so important, my boy."

"Why?"

"Because someone claims to have found the entrance to Ophir."

"Who?"

"A German archaeologist named Heinrich Schliemann."

When I give him a blank stare, he pronounces the name once again—slowly.

"HINE-rick SHLEE-mun."

"He found it? Really?"

Uncle Arthur shrugs. "Nobody's sure yet. He'll unveil his discoveries tonight at the museum. The members of AWE will all be assembling there. We need to authenticate his claims as quickly as possible because there's something else."

"What?"

"Besides all the treasure that's buried in Ophir, it's also supposedly the final resting place of an ancient artifact known as the Ruby Tablet."

"Wow! What's on it?"

"A recipe."

I make a face. That's not what I thought he would say.

"A recipe?" I repeat. "For what?"

He leans in closer, then he whispers, "For gold."

"For *gold*?" I exclaim.

"Yes. The recipe for making gold is supposedly written on the Ruby Tablet. Legend says that's how the ancient Ophirians had so much gold. They didn't mine it—they *made* it. Mixed it up like cake batter!"

"Whoa!"

Uncle Arthur nods. "Now, if the legend is true, and the Ruby Tablet does exist, it would be the most powerful artifact ever found. Whoever finds it first would become . . ."

"The richest person on earth!" I whisper.

He nods and smiles at me. "AZ, I've been trying to solve this ancient mystery for my entire life, since I was about your age. But it's remained a puzzle. A puzzle no one has ever solved. But tonight, we just might find the very first piece."

THE ALLIANCE

S ingh lands us at Heathrow Airport. I was asleep, and his landing was so smooth, I didn't even feel it. Uncle Arthur shakes me awake and tells me to get my things. I decide to leave my duffel bag and take my bright-yellow backpack.

As we duck through the small oval doorway and make our way down the portable staircase, Singh jumps out of a window in the cockpit. With a cool gymnastic flip, he lands neatly on the tarmac, just as a long black limo pulls up. The driver of the limo gets out, tipping his shiny black hat toward Singh. In turn, Singh bows his big red turban. We hit the bottom of the stairs, and Singh smoothly steps over to open the rear passenger door just as we're arriving.

Getting in the limo, Uncle Arthur nods at the silent Sikh. "Thank you, Singh!"

Singh nods slightly.

As I get in the car, I quickly stammer, "Um, uh, thank you, Singh."

CHAPTER THREE

He gives me a small nod as well.

Singh steers the limo through the busy streets of London. Soon, we arrive at the British Museum. It looks like a big white palace with towering grooved pillars. Crowds teem outside, and camera crews huddle around the doors. Singh pulls into the special VIP underground parking lot and lets us out.

I usually don't like dumb museums. My parents are always dragging me to them. They're boring, and you can't touch anything. Once I made a list of things that might make museums more interesting for kids.

After we manage to muscle our way into the museum, we're ushered through the security line. Not one but five armed security guards fail to notice I'm carrying a big yellow backpack containing over a dozen items the museum specifically bans. Maybe I get through because the room is so crowded. Or maybe it's because Uncle Arthur went around greeting all the guards and thumping them on the back until they almost fell over. Also, I think security guards hate searching kids, especially bigger kids wearing baggy clothes. They can't tell contraband bumps from weird body-fat lumps without making you take your shirt off. And that's a lose-lose situation either way.

Uncle Arthur and I hurry down long corridors with vaulted ceilings. We finally reach the museum's Egyptian wing, a grand room packed with excited guests talking to one another and drinking champagne. A string quartet performs by the podium. Above them hangs a large gold banner that reads:

OPHIR
THE LOST CITY OF SECRETS

Uncle Arthur grabs me by the shoulder. He maneuvers me through the crowd until we reach a large group of guests who

Ways to Improve Museums

1) No shirt, no shoes? No problem!
2) Let people touch the art.
3) And taste it. A statue might taste like grape soda and how would we know?
4) They only need two sections in the museum: Interesting/DUMB Put cool stuff—mummies & swords & polar bears—in "Interesting" section. Then put all the paintings and old furniture in the "Dumb" section. Saves time.
5) Skateboarding should be allowed on all floors. People will see more that way
6) Put GPS chips inside museum statues in case they're walking around at night trying to escape.

all immediately disperse upon our arrival. That is, everyone leaves except for an ancient-looking man wearing a regal navy coat with brass buttons. Uncle Arthur introduces him as Lord Weatherhead, executive director of the museum.

Lord Weatherhead looks a million years old. When I shake his hand, I catch a whiff of peppermint and foot powder. He's wearing an Alliance ring just like Uncle Arthur's, only his has a large blue diamond sunk in the center. I wonder what it could mean. I want to ask, but Lord Weatherhead and my uncle are already deep in conversation.

I let them confer privately while I scan the room for other Alliance members wearing gold rings. I'm lost in concentration when a dark figure appears beside me and nearly startles me into needing a new pair of adventure pants.

"Pardon me, but who are *you*?" a sharp, irritated voice says.

I turn around, and I'm confused at first. I think the person standing before me must be a small butler or something because he's wearing a tuxedo. Then I realize he's way too short to be a butler. Actually, he's the same age as I am. He peers at me with piercing blue eyes through his thick square glasses.

"Who *are* you?" he repeats. "Don't you know who you are?"

"I'm, um . . . AZ."

He frowns. "Were you invited?"

"Was I invited? How should I know? Were *you*?"

Tuxedo Kid scoffs indignantly. "I am *Edward Weatherhead*, grandson of Lord Weatherhead. And I was definitely invited to tonight's event, because I'm invited to every event at the museum."

Big whoopee-ding. I just hook a thumb at my uncle and say, "Well, he was invited, and I came with him."

"You came with . . . Sir Arthur?"

"I call him *Uncle* Arthur."

"Oh, you're Sir Arthur's nephew?" He puts on a phony smile. "I'm so sorry for the confusion, but I had to ask. This is a very high-security event, and, well, you don't exactly look like you were invited."

"Oh, I don't? Well, at least I don't look like an emperor penguin."

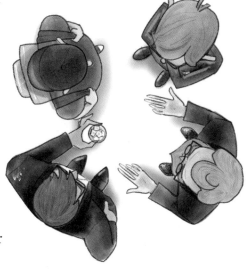

His eyes go wide, and his nostrils flare. "Your outfit is completely inappropriate!" he shoots back. "You look like a rejected extra in a hip-hop video!"

"You look like an orchestra conductor."

Lord Weatherhead turns around and interrupts us. "So, you've met!" He smiles. "AZ, this is my grandson, Edward. He's twelve too."

Lord Weatherhead clamps his spotty claw on Edward's shoulder and smiles at me with a pair of misty blue eyes.

"AZ, my boy, I apologize, but I must take your uncle Arthur away for a moment. We have important matters to discuss. Edward will escort you through the exhibition."

Edward lets out an almost inaudible gasp, then catches himself and nods.

I attempt a protest. "I don't need an escort, but I do need some grub!"

Lord Weatherhead tilts his head. "Pardon?"

"Grub," I repeat, patting my round belly. "Food! I'm

hungry enough to eat a bear."

Edward snickers. "Looks like you already did."

"My nephew is hungry," Uncle Arthur says, joining the conversation. "A dominant character trait, I'm afraid."

Lord Weatherhead smiles. "Well, there's nothing wrong with a little hunger! Keeps a young man sharp."

"He seems pretty dull to me," Edward mumbles.

"An impressive dinner awaits you, young man," Lord Weatherhead assures me. "Edward, please bring AZ to the banquet hall before you go anywhere else."

"But, Grandfather—I'm to show Mr. Schliemann to the podium!"

Lord Weatherhead's face darkens. "*Herr* Schliemann, Edward. We use the proper Germanic title. Herr Schliemann."

Edward flares his nostrils. "Of course, Grandfather."

"Now run along, you two." Lord Weatherhead smiles fondly at us both before turning and walking away with Uncle Arthur.

Everyone thinks all kids will get along. Since Edward and I are both twelve years old, people assume we'll naturally be friends and won't want to beat the living tar out of each other.

Wrong.

Edward is a big know-it-all loudmouth who corrects nearly everything I say. He knows everything there is to know about *everything*. He's worked at the museum with his grandfather for *blah-diddy-blah* years. He's studied with every *whoopee-ding* expert and can read all the *whatchamacallit* hieroglyphs ever found.

Big deal. I can make a foam bomb. I can also eat twice my weight in ham, which I offer to show him in the banquet hall.

Unfortunately, there's no ham in the banquet hall. It's all Egyptian food. Servers are floating around with trays of figs, fresh-baked flatbreads, and petite lamb chops dripping with mint sauce.

Edward and I position ourselves at a tall table and wait for the food to come our way. I take everything they'll give me. I'm a bit bummed that each *tiny* plate contains only one *miniscule* piece of food, so I manage to convince the guy with the lamb chops to give me five helpings. My plates cover the entire table.

This, of course, mortifies Edward. "Have enough food?" he sneers.

"What?" I shrug. "It's not my fault they're little plates."

Just then, I notice a silver bowl sitting on the table. It's filled with sugary green gumdrops. I grab a big handful and stuff them in my pocket. Then I grab another handful.

"For good measure," I tell Edward.

That's when Sir Edward the Egghead balls up his little fists, ready to sound off on my etiquette again. But then he suddenly lets out a little yelp when a girl approaches us.

"Oh, hello, Lux!" He starts coughing and trying to compose himself even though his face is as red as a boiled lobster.

"Hi, Edward," the girl says.

She has long wavy black hair with vibrant red tips. She's wearing a sparkly silver dress and shoes that match. I can feel my face go red when she looks at me.

"So?" she says to Edward. "What's up?"

Edward stammers some nonsensical gibberish that ends with, "You scared me!"

Then he introduces me to Lux Lopez, the thirteen-year-old daughter of Lorenzo Lopez, an esteemed AWE explorer specializing in underwater excavations. Lux and her dad came all the way from their home in California. Her family—her parents, herself, and her four brothers—splits time between San Diego and Baja California Sur, Mexico, for her dad's work.

"Who's this?" she asks, nodding at me.

Edward shrugs. "I have no idea."

I try to laugh and say something funny. But just then, one of my lamb chops slips from my fingers and falls, splattering mint sauce all over the shiny marble floor. I hurry to pick it up but accidentally kick it across the room. It finally lands on some old guy's shoe.

"Perfect," Edward says with a sigh. "Just perfect."

My cheeks burn with embarrassment. I quickly turn around before the old guy sees me.

Lux tugs on my arm. "Look!" she says, gesturing toward the man. "He didn't even notice!"

I turn my head and peek at the old guy. He's still talking away to a group of ladies. He seems completely unaware that I just attacked him with an appetizer.

"I bet he goes home with it still on his shoe," Lux says, giggling.

"Not if I have anything to do with it!" Edward says. He straightens his vest, preparing to cross the room and alert the victim of my wayward lamb chop.

"Edward!" Lux stops him. "Don't you *dare*."

He pauses.

"I mean it!" she hisses. "Come back here right now."

"*Fine!*" He sulks back to the table. "I guess we'll just encourage food fights in a museum, then."

Lux smiles at me.

"Um . . . want a gumdrop?" I have no idea what else to say.

She takes a single green gumdrop from the small cluster in my palm. She pops it into her mouth.

"I love gumdrops," she says. "So chewy!"

I smile and try to pop a gumdrop in my mouth too. I miss. The little green gumdrop goes sailing over my shoulder. I look

over at Lux quickly.

She laughs and extends her hand. "I never got your name."

I smile at her again and open my mouth—only I can't remember my name. My mind is completely blank.

Edward cuts in. "His name—if you can call it that—is AZ."

"Oh?" Lux looks at me, curious. "And what does AZ stand for?"

I stare silently back at Lux. My mind is still blank. Lux reaches for another gumdrop as she waits for me to respond.

"Don't fill up on candy, you two," Edward interrupts.

"Why not?" I ask, suddenly able to speak again. I attempt to toss another gumdrop at my mouth. This one hits me right in the eye.

"Because a pharaonic feast awaits you!"

He leads us over to a banquet table overflowing with even more food. I eye the succulent platters of roasted meat and big baskets of bread. I excitedly stuff the green gumdrops back into my pocket.

"What's over there?" I ask, pointing to an elegant buffet table with a sign that reads:

Pharaonic Foods

"Pharaonic foods are the foods pharaohs ate," Edward explains. "Tonight's guest of honor, Heinrich, specifically chose the menu. He's eaten food from all around the world, so we had to be careful to get everything just right. One chef was even fired over his ostrich eggs!"

I grab a plate. "The pharaohs ate this?"

"*Only* the pharaohs ate this food," he explains. "These are all royal recipes, taken from the hieroglyphs found in the royal tombs of the pharaohs."

"So, what did everybody else eat?" Lux asks.

"Well, you know . . ." Edward shrugs in my general direction. "Commoners ate . . . common things."

I look at him. "Did you just gesture toward me when you said 'commoners'?"

"I don't think so." He delicately spoons a single fig onto his plate.

"Yes, you did. I saw you. You waved your hand at me like I was a commoner."

"Did I?" Edward hands the plate to Lux. "You must try the stuffed figs," he tells her. "They're heaven."

I decide to ignore Little Lord Loudmouth. I focus on loading up my plate with everything it will hold. Stuffed figs, roasted duck, braised quail, sweet little honey cakes. Man, I can't believe how well those pharaohs ate!

Edward tells us the ancient Egyptians developed sophisticated tastes as their trade routes spread out farther and farther. This brought in all kinds of exotic delicacies, strange meats, pungent spices, and fragrant fruit trees. But only the pharaohs got to sample these new discoveries.

Lux scoops some fava bean salad onto her plate and sighs. "That doesn't seem fair. Imagine being a little kid seeing all those mysterious animals and fruit trees arrive and knowing you'd never touch or taste any of it."

"Well, they didn't exactly let the commoners *starve*." Edward gestures toward my loaded plate. "They ate onions, grains, fatty mutton—"

"What's *fatty mutton*?" Lux wrinkles her nose. "Sounds gross."

"It's just cheap meat," Edward explains. "We'd throw it in the garbage. But the less privileged citizens were just like you, AZ. They'd eat anything."

CHAPTER THREE

I can feel my face getting hot with frustration.

We come to the end of the buffet line. It's time to eat or keep arguing with Edward. Luckily, my hunger wins out as I dig into the pharaonic feast heaped on my plate.

The truth is . . . I *have* eaten a lot of garbage—literally. It's usually on a dare or for a bet, but I find perfectly good food in the trash at school all the time. Kids throw away sandwiches, apples, pickle wedges wrapped in waxed paper. It all stays edible for days and days after. Nondairy pudding cups live for weeks past their expiration dates. Packaged string cheese is almost indestructible.

Oh, and candy—candy is forever. Candy cannot die. Old chocolate bars, stale peanut butter cups, broken candy canes, Red Hots from last Halloween, sour balls that rolled under the radiator, red licorice vines that fell between the couch cushions. I don't care where it came from or how old it is. Candy can come back to life.

Just dump all your old candy into a glass bowl and nuke it in the microwave. Wait until everything melts together into a sticky, sludgy puddle of goo. Then pour it over ice cream for a weird-tasting sundae or into an empty ice cube tray to make your own mystery-flavored candy bars.

I've eaten plenty of other things Edward never could. Like when Dad brought home a rattlesnake from his dig in Arizona. He cut the snake lengthwise and pan-seared it in a chipotle-butter sauce. He thought the snake would taste like chicken, but it tasted more like a soft-boiled bike tire pan-seared in chipotle-butter sauce. Mom gagged on the first bite, and Dad turned a weird shade of green halfway through. I was the only one who finished everything on my plate. Iron-gut AZ, that's me.

I pick up a stuffed fig. "So, only pharaohs ate this?"

Edward nods. "And their families."

"Good." I grab another plate and start loading it up with more food. "Because if my dad were the pharaoh and ate way better food than everybody else, I would totally revolt."

Lux giggles, which makes Edward's big ears turn bright pink.

"Lux, why didn't you take any roasted gazelle? It's divine," says Edward.

"Gross." Lux wrinkles her nose. "You think I'd eat that?"

"Why not?"

She looks at him incredulously. "Because I don't eat meat, Edward, and you know that."

"Oh, right. Of course."

She looks disgusted. "I'm a vegetarian. I haven't eaten meat since I was nine."

Edward coughs, and his ears go one shade darker.

Suddenly, the piercing sound of microphone feedback screeches through the air. We hear Lord Weatherhead's voice.

Startled, Edward wheels around to see his grandfather standing at the podium with a man and a woman. "Ugh! I knew I should have shown them to the podium!" He rushes off toward the main gallery, where the string quartet has stopped playing.

"C'mon!" Lux tugs my sleeve. "It's starting!"

As we hurry out of the banquet hall, I manage to skillfully shove a few lamb chops into the greasy-food pocket of my adventure pants. The pocket is lined with plastic wrap.

We join the excited throng gathered under the big gold banner that reads: OPHIR. Lord Weatherhead stands in front of a thick red velvet curtain. He clears his throat into the microphone, sending another painful screech through the air.

"I would like to thank everyone for coming. I especially

would like to thank Heinrich Schliemann for sharing his amazing finds—treasures that very well may be from the Lost City of Secrets, the ancient Egyptian city of Ophir."

Everyone applauds.

"And without further ado, I introduce tonight's guests of honor, Herr Heinrich Schliemann and his wife, Greta."

The crowd applauds for Heinrich Schliemann as he steps in front of the red velvet curtain and takes the microphone. I dislike him at once. He's a weasel-faced man wearing a baggy suit and thick black eyeglasses that sit crookedly on his pasty white face. He grins wolfishly at the crowd, licking his lips quickly, just like a lizard.

His wife, Greta, is a whale of a woman. She wears a bulging putrid-green dress, and her shrewd little black eyes float like twin raisins at the center of her large, doughy face. Her black hair is pulled up tight and piled at the top of her head like oily black sausages.

Heinrich smiles. "Thank you for zee chance to be here tonight," he says in his thick accent. "I have waited a lifetime for a discovery as important as this. Zee artifacts I will share tonight include a gold crown, an ivory scepter, and a jewel-encrusted knife, all believed to be from Ophir."

"Where is Ophir?" somebody in the crowd shouts.

Heinrich chuckles. "Well, I can't tell you that, can I? I can say zee lost city is located on zee island of Cyprus, but I can say no more."

The crowd breaks out in excited gasps.

Heinrich continues. "Whenever King Solomon traveled to Ophir, he was guarded by zee entire Phoenician army. And just as King Solomon did, I must keep myself and zee site protected. If zee location were to be revealed, thousands of people would flock to see zee vast treasures, emerald roads, and silver ships that sailed on Ophir's legendary pink lake. And that would no doubt damage zee site."

"What about the Ruby Tablet?" someone else shouts. "Did you find the Ruby Tablet?"

"We have uncovered only zee very smallest part of zee ancient city. It will take time to uncover zee rest. That said, I myself believe zee legend of zee Ruby Tablet is only that: a legend."

The crowd murmurs.

"Now," he says, "zee time has come for me to share my discoveries with you, my dear, dear friends! I give you zee treasures of Ophir!"

Suddenly, the giant red curtain behind him falls back. The crowd gasps. The exhibition hall positively glows from all the gold artifacts inside. The audience explodes in applause, stampeding into the exhibit hall, dazzled by the treasures.

Lux, Edward, and I are carried along with the crowd. We have to struggle to get through the excited throngs, pushing our way to see the Ophirian treasures. Many of the ancient gold artifacts are jewel encrusted. Each one is more splendid than the last. I can tell they are very expensive treasures, probably priceless.

"Ophir was famous for its emeralds," Edward says as we gaze at large chunks of the precious green stone. "Its roads were even made of solid emerald!"

Next, he shows us a case with several large chunks of ruby, another famous gemstone from Ophir. There's also a large artist's rendering of what the Ruby Tablet might look like.

"I read that the Ruby Tablet is over seven feet tall," Edward says.

Lux nods. "I heard people who touch it turn to stone."

I search my brain for a Ruby Tablet factoid. "Um, I heard it's made of solid ruby!"

Edward turns to me with a vicious look.

My cheeks turn red.

"Really?" he says. "The Ruby Tablet is made of *ruby*, you say? How amazing! However did you know that?"

I feel like an idiot. The worst part is, he's *not* an idiot. He knows something about almost everything.

He shows us a case containing a small shard from a much larger ancient clay pot. "See that symbol stamped at the bottom?" he asks. "The crooked arrow inside a circle? That's the official stamp of Ophir. It's the first artifact anyone's ever found that had Ophir's stamp. It's proof the city existed."

I snort at the shard. "That little brown lump is proof? It looks like a lump of ancient dog poo."

Lux giggles.

"It's a priceless artifact," Edward snaps.

I shrug. "Still looks like dog poo."

Undeterred, Edward shows us another case filled with little blue stone statues called *shabtis*. They were put in the tombs of royalty, and they supposedly came to life once the tomb was sealed.

"The idea was that the shabtis would wake up and run around doing whatever their master told them to do," says Edward.

"Cool!" Lux says. "I'd make my shabtis clean everything. I hate cleaning."

"Yeah!" I nod. "And they could do all your homework too!"

"Of course." Edward rolls his eyes. "Because everyone knows there's homework in the afterworld."

My cheeks turn red again. "All I meant was—"

"What are those over there?" Lux asks, cutting me off.

"Those?" Edward looks over to where she's pointing. "Funeral knives. Used to prepare the mummies before they went into their tombs."

"What's that hook thing?" Lux asks.

"That's a brain-scooping hook," Edward explains. "They inserted it through your nostril and poked it up into your brain. Then they scooped the brain out."

"Nasty!" She grimaces.

"Cool!" I nod.

Edward smiles at me. "Luckily, the process wouldn't take very long in your case, AZ."

"Hey! Are you saying my brain is—"

"AZ!" someone shouts from across the room.

I turn to look. It's Uncle Arthur, making his way through the crowd with Lord Weatherhead. They both have worried looks on their faces.

"Looks like trouble," Lux whispers.

"There you are!" shouts Uncle Arthur. "I've been looking for you everywhere! The Alliance has called an emergency meeting downstairs," he quickly explains. "Can I leave you alone for an hour or so? I don't want to come back here and find you've been behaving like a wild monkey or been kidnapped." He frowns. "Quite frankly, I don't want to do the paperwork."

"I'll be fine," I tell him.

"Plus, we'll watch over him!" Lux says with a smile. "Right, Edward?"

Edward sniffs haughtily.

I watch as Uncle Arthur disappears down the hall, followed by several distinguished-looking guests. They are all wearing gold octagon-shaped rings. That's when I realize I still have Uncle Arthur's Alliance ring on my finger.

"Uncle Arthur!" I shout out, but he's too far away to hear me.

"So, what do you think, AZ? Are these really treasures from Ophir?" asks Lux.

"Well—"

"Definitely," Edward cuts in before I can answer. "My grandfather is 99 percent sure, and so am I. Obviously, they—"

"Sorry." This time, Lux cuts in on Edward. "But I asked AZ."

Finally, it's Edward's turn to be embarrassed. His big soup-bowl-handle ears turn an even brighter shade of pink.

"I dunno," I tell them, shaking my head. "Something's not right."

"What?" Lux asks.

"Just a gut feeling," I say.

"Must be a lot in your gut, judging by the size of it,"

Edward mumbles.

Luckily, Lux doesn't hear him.

"One thing's for sure," she says. "Heinrich really wants to join the Alliance. My dad told me he's been trying to get invited for over three years."

I look at her. "Something tells me he'll never be invited."

"Well, that *is* disappointing," someone says in a thick German accent.

We whirl around to see Heinrich standing there with his wife, Greta.

Edward tries to backpedal. "Um . . . ah . . . excellent show, sir! Tr-truly!" he stammers. "The artifacts you brought to the museum are fascinating! No matter what their origin!" he hastily adds.

"Is that so?" Heinrich says.

"Oh yes. Quite," Edward says, his ears almost purple now. "And I would know. I'm Lord Weatherhead's grandson."

"I see," Heinrich says, licking his lips. "So then, you know all about zee museum?"

"I know *everything* about the museum!" Edward says proudly.

"Even your grandfather's secret room?"

"Um . . . pardon me?"

"Your grandfather's secret room," Heinrich repeats. "Have you seen it?"

"I don't . . . I . . ." Edward stammers. Finally, he says, "No such room exists."

"Well, I think it does exist," Heinrich says. "In fact, I *know* it does."

"Impossible!" Edward says. "Grandfather never lets anybody into the—" Then he catches himself. He clears his throat. "What I mean is, I'm sorry, but you're quite mistaken."

"And you." Heinrich turns to me. "I see you're wearing an

Alliance ring on your finger. Very impressive for one so young to be a member."

"He's not a member," Edward corrects quickly as Heinrich leers at the ring on my finger.

I involuntarily shove my hands behind my back.

"I myself have wanted to wear such a ring for some time now," Heinrich says, smiling. "Some people would sell a ring like that for a great deal of money."

"Not—not me," I say with a gasp. "I would never sell it."

"I see." Heinrich nods. "Pity. Well, then, children, I bid you a good evening." Heinrich bows.

His enormous wife glares at us without speaking.

As soon as they're gone, Edward pulls us to the side and starts whispering rapidly. "You're right, AZ. Something *is* wrong. Nobody's supposed to know about the secret room."

"Wait," I say, confused. "Is this secret room where the members are meeting right now?"

Edward shakes his head. "No. The secret room is . . . is . . . well, it's a secret!"

"Then how does Heinrich know about it?" Lux asks.

"Do you think he's been in there?" I ask.

Edward gasps. "He couldn't!"

"Then how does he know about it?"

Edward puts his hands to his temples, trying to think of possible answers. "He might have . . . Or maybe he . . ." Finally, he shakes his head. "No! It's impossible! He couldn't get ahold of the . . . It would be impossible to . . . Heavens!"

"I've never even heard about the secret room," Lux says. "Never."

"It's where Grandfather keeps his—no!" Edward stops himself. He looks sadly at Lux. "I'm sorry—I can't tell you anything. I can't!"

"Well, secret or no secret, I think we should make sure it's safe," Lux says.

"Yeah." I nod. "And quick. Maybe Heinrich's headed there right now!"

Edward looks as if he might explode. "But I can't take you there!" he says. "I'll get into a lot of trouble if Grandfather finds out I've even told you about the secret room!"

"But *you* didn't tell us about it. Heinrich did," Lux says calmly. "Look—we know something's up. The secret room could be at risk. And no one else is here to make sure it's secure."

He sighs. "Then I'll have to go alone," he says.

"Alone? What if Heinrich is waiting for you?" she asks.

"No! You can't come! If I ever took someone there, my grandfather would . . . I can't! No! Positively not!"

He gives us a tortured look. I can almost hear the wheels spinning in his head: he knows he shouldn't bring anyone to the secret room, yet he also knows he shouldn't go alone. He'd better decide fast, though, because if Heinrich somehow finds a way into the secret room, it could be devastating!

At last, Edward flares his nostrils and squares his shoulders. "All right," he says. "Let's go. We must secure Grandfather's secret room together. But I warn you—this is never to be spoken of again. Understood?"

"Perfectly," Lux says.

"You got it, Ed." I nod.

Edward glares at me, then takes off. We follow as he quickly leads us out of the main hall, down a marble staircase, and through several rooms filled with medieval artifacts. Then he stops short.

Edward looks over his shoulder before pulling aside an old tapestry, revealing a small ancient-looking door. He takes an old skeleton key from his pocket and unlocks it.

We walk down a creaking old flight of stairs, heading to a stone wall with an iron door.

"Whatever you do, don't touch anything," Edward says.

He removes another key and unlocks the iron door. Then we step inside. It's dark and dusty smelling. Edward turns on a light.

"If Grandfather ever finds out I let you in here . . ." He seems even more nervous than usual.

"He won't find out," Lux says for the millionth time.

The room is crowded with all sorts of odd, not-especially-interesting-looking objects lined up on shelves.

"What is this place?" Lux whispers.

Edward struggles to answer. "It's . . . it's where Grandfather keeps anything he feels needs research or repairs."

I stumble over a big brass telescope, which goes rolling across the floor. I go to pick it back up, but Edward lunges for it, nearly knocking me over.

"No! You *mustn't* touch anything in here!" He sounds frantic.

"Oh, stop it already, Edward," Lux says. "It's not like we're going to break something."

"No!" Edward shakes his head in panic. "You don't understand. The things in here are—"

"Hey, look!" I squint into the shadowy shelves. "Is that another bowl of gumdrops?"

I walk over to a small blue bowl filled with green gumdrops. The bowl is sitting next to a weird camera. I pop a few gumdrops toward my mouth, and for the first time, they make it in.

"Ooh, wintergreen," I say. Then I pick up the camera. "What's this thing?"

"It's an old stereopticon," Lux says. "It's also called a *magic lantern.* It was the first 3-D camera ever made. People said it brought pictures to life."

"Weird," I say. I bring the viewfinder up to my eyes.

"Give me that!" Edward snaps. "Don't touch that!"

I reach out my arm to hold the stereopticon up and away, so he can't reach it.

"I said give me that!" Edward says, jumping for it. "It's not yours! Give it here!"

I hold the stereopticon up higher and keep peering through the viewfinder. "Hey, there's a picture in here!"

"A picture of what?" Lux asks. "Let me see."

Squinting through the viewfinder, I see the image of a flowing river. It's so lifelike it almost seems real. The waves seem to be rippling in the water. I swear the crooked palm tree up on the beach is swaying in the wind. There are words in small print beneath the image. I focus in to read them.

CHAPTER THREE

"Put that down immediately!" Edward exclaims, getting louder. "You have no idea what it—"

"It says, 'The Nile River, 1930'!" I read aloud.

"I said, put that down!" Edward shouts. He grabs me and roughly pulls down my arm, knocking us right into Lux.

Then the room goes black.

I feel as though I'm falling in open air. I reach out for Lux, but she's gone. I try to shout, but my voice doesn't work. I try to touch my face, but it's not there. I'm falling in total darkness, devoid of sight, sound, taste, smell, and touch.

Then I start spinning. A rumbling vibration surges through me. I feel a tremendous pressure on my chest and the sensation of speed. I'm rocketing faster and faster downward, and there seems to be nothing below.

THE ACCIDENTAL EXPLORERS

W *hoooomph!*

I finally land. And land hard.

I hear water. Birdcalls fill the thick, humid air. I feel warm, gritty sand beneath my fingertips. I try to open my eyes, but the brilliant sunshine stings them. A splitting pain rips through my head. Squinting painfully, I take a deep breath, count to three, and manage to sit up. I shade my face with my hands and peek out.

I'm on a beach. I don't see Edward or Lux anywhere.

The beach is beside a wide, quickly flowing river. Across the river is a thick mat of green jungle, with tangled vines woven around fragrant blooming trees. I smell eucalyptus, cypress, and sycamore. Down by the river are tall reeds and papyrus. The river itself is covered with floating carpets of bright-green lily pads dotted by pink and white lotus flowers.

From the dense thicket of jungle behind me, I hear a groan. The shrubbery rustles. Edward crawls out slowly, his tuxedo torn and dirty, his sandy-brown hair messed up, and his glasses askew. He looks as if he flew through a tornado.

Edward! I'm actually relieved to see him!

He glares at me. "You moron!" he shouts. "I told you not to touch anything!"

Never mind. I take that back.

I stare up at him and blink. "Got it." I look around in confusion. "Where *are* we?"

Edward smooths back his damp hair. "How should I know?" he snaps. "What did the bloody photo say on the stereopticon?"

"It said, 'The Nile River, 1930.' "

"Well, then, that's where we probably are—the Nile River . . . in 1930."

"How do you know?"

"Pick it up and see for yourself," he snaps, pointing to my feet.

There, I see the stereopticon half-buried in the sand. I quickly pick it up and peer through the lens. He's right. The photo in the camera is identical to the scene in front of us. Same beach, same wide, rippling river, same crooked palm tree swaying in the wind.

"How do we know it's 1930, though?" I ask. "Maybe we just transported to the Nile but didn't go back in time."

Edward stares at me as if I'm bonkers. "Areas along the present-day Nile are heavily populated. But as you can see, there's nothing here! Also, the present-day Nile is surrounded by sand and rock. We're in the middle of a jungle!"

"Oh," I say. He has a point.

As I gaze all around, it starts to hit me. I can't believe it—we're sitting by the Nile River in 1930! A grin crosses my face.

Edward is not as excited about the situation as I am. He's furious.

"*You* did this!" he shouts, pointing a finger at me. "*You* brought us here!"

"Me?" I shoot back at him. "Well, *you* brought us to the secret room!"

"I didn't know you'd monkey with every single thing you saw! I told you not to—"

"There you are!" a voice says.

We turn to see Lux stumble out of the jungle, her hair messy, her dress ripped, her face smudged with dirt. "What... what happened?"

Edward and I simultaneously point at each other and shout, "He did it!"

After we all calm down, Edward tells us what he thinks happened. Over time, the Alliance has discovered quite a few artifacts that appear to have mystical abilities—strange powers that can't be explained by science. Whenever an artifact seems dangerous or unexplainable or both, the Alliance stores it in the secret room.

Edward had never seen the stereopticon before, so he didn't fully understand its powers. But as we just discovered, it can transport people to a place shown in the photograph inside the viewfinder.

"It probably brought all three of us here because we were touching," Edward said. "Remember? I grabbed your shoulder right as you were reading the name of the Nile River out loud, and we fell into Lux."

"So how do we get back?" I ask.

"Isn't it obvious, genius?" Edward says angrily. "The

stereopticon transports you wherever and whenever the picture shows."

Lux stares at me, then back at Edward. "So, we need a picture of the British Museum?"

Edward nods. "I believe so."

"But we don't have a photo of the museum," I say.

"Well, then, we'll have to find one, won't we?"

Edward puts his glasses back on, but now they're bent and crooked. Lux and I just look at each other. We're all silent for a moment, and I suddenly notice how loud the flowing river is.

Then a big yellow butterfly lands on Edward's hand. He shrieks, slapping at the air and jumping around as if a swarm of killer bees were attacking him.

I roll my eyes at him, which only makes him madder.

"When we get back, I'm telling them you broke the museum rules!" Edward says.

"Oh, go shove your museum rules up your—"

"All right," Lux interrupts with a sigh. "Maybe we should start by inventorying our gear."

Gear! I should've thought of that!

Lux plants her sparkly shoe on a tree stump. "I have my Tecpatl knife," she says. She reaches down and whips out an ornate dagger from a concealed compartment in the sole of her shoe. "I have all my shoes outfitted to carry my knife," she explains.

"Why on earth do you carry a *knife* everywhere?" Edward asks.

"Because," she says with a sniff, "I believe having a knife is better than *not* having one. Especially this one. It's an Aztecan ceremonial knife. The double-edged blade is made from sharpened flint, and the handle is carved out of wood. I can carry it anywhere without setting off metal detectors. Plus, the blade can be used to ignite a spark in an emergency."

"Is it sharp?" I ask.

In a flash, she whips the knife at a nearby tree. *Wissssh-uk!* It punctures a coconut, and clear sweet juice runs down its side.

"It's sharp enough." She grins.

I'm starting to understand that Lux is a very special kind of girl.

It's my turn to inventory my gear. I start sorting through the contents of my backpack.

"I have a cell phone!" I grab it and turn it on. No signal. Zilch. "It's not working," I announce.

"Perhaps it's because there are no cell phone towers in 1930," Edward says, rolling his eyes.

Ignoring him, I spot my portable GPS unit. "Check it out! We can use my GPS to figure out where we are!"

"Great!" Lux says, looking at me expectantly.

Meanwhile, Edward buries his face in his hands and groans.

"Oh no," I whisper as I inspect the device.

Lux frowns. "What is it?"

I hold up the GPS unit and shake it. "It's . . . it's broken."

"Broken?"

"The screen is cracked."

"Oh," she says sadly.

Edward groans again from behind his hands. "Who cares if it's broken?" he exclaims, his hands now waving in the air. "Don't you get it? It wouldn't work anyway! GPS relies on satellite signals. But it's 1930—there are no satellites!"

Without a word, I shove the useless GPS into my backpack. Once again, he's right. He's always right.

Edward sniffs. "Plus, we don't need fancy gadgets to get our bearings."

"You and my dad would really get along," I snarl.

"All we need is a compass," Edward says. He takes out a gold compass from his vest pocket and flips it open. He peers around, continuing to survey our surroundings and consult his compass.

"See that rock protrusion over there?" He points at a rounded low mountaintop. "I think that is the Sabaluka pluton. It's unique to the sixth cataract of the Nile. I remember reading about it in the ancient Sudanese exhibit at the museum."

I stare at him dumfounded as he continues.

"The pluton is just north of us, and the Nile is flowing in that direction. So I believe we are somewhere in the Sudan desert, north of Khartoum."

Edward bends down and draws a map in the sand. I carefully copy the map in my Adventure Journal, just in case.

I sit down on the hot sandy beach and sulk, trying not to think about the argument I had with Dad about why it's important to pay attention in school. I have the creeping suspicion Dad may have been right. Maybe you do need some book smarts to be an explorer. Technology can't do *everything*. Actually, technology can't do *anything* for us right now.

I pull out one more thing from my backpack: iodine tablets for water purification. "I have these," I say sullenly. They're the only thing making me *not* look like the biggest jerk in the world right now. But no one seems to be paying much attention, so I decide to stop inventorying.

"OK," Lux says. "Let's prioritize. We need water, food, and fire."

I jump up and shout, "Food! Amen!"

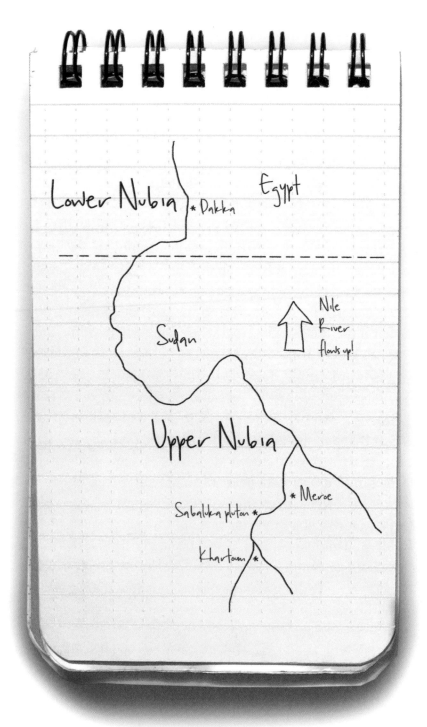

Edward rolls his eyes.

We head into the jungle. Lux uses her Tecpatl knife to hack down green coconuts and some sturdy vines. She knots the vines around the coconuts, so we can sling them over our shoulders like canteens. Edward rummages for firewood. I, meanwhile, have declared myself the *official chef* of this accidental expedition. I look for different ingredients, which I stick into my backpack.

I find lots of stuff. There are plenty of cattails. You can roast them over an open fire and eat the sticky caramel center. You can also boil them whole and eat them like corn on the cob. I also find a date tree with a bunch of ripe dates and a mulberry bush with at least ten handfuls of ripe berries. I grab some lotus flowers too. They are actually edible. I stuff my pockets with as much as I can.

As I pass by a hollowed-out tree, I see some movement. Grubs! They're edible as well. I pull out a bug jar from my backpack and fill it with wriggling white wormlike bug larvae. There are also some centipedes crawling around. Those will be just as tasty. I fill another jar with them.

As I scoop up the last of the creepy-but-nutritious crawlies, a flash of brilliant green stops me. It's a tiny poison dart frog. Natives used to coat the tips of their arrows with the poisonous mucus this frog secretes. I carefully back away from it.

I'm just about to shout at Edward to come and see the frog when I hear him yelp. He slaps a mosquito on his arm.

"The insects out here are enormous!" he says.

"And a lot of them are edible!" I grin.

"The ancient Egyptians hated insects," he says. "That's why they shaved their heads and wore wigs. King Pepi II even walked around with naked slaves who were smeared with honey."

I wrinkle my face. "Why honey?"

"So flies would land on the slaves and not on him."

"I don't think flies like honey. Do they?"

"Well, it's a historical fact," he tells me flatly. "You should open a book sometime."

"And you should test the things your books say before you believe them. I know—why don't you strip naked and smear some honey on yourself? Then you can see if flies show up."

He snorts. "Very clever."

By late afternoon, Edward and I have piled our bounty on the beach, where we find that Lux has also collected a bunch of coconuts. I look around for her, and then I hear her shouting in the distance. We head over to her.

"I found a boat," she says.

"A boat?" I repeat.

She nods and shows us down in the reeds where a small white wooden skiff is nestled in the marsh grass. "Now we can sail down the river!" she says.

"I am not sailing down any river," Edward informs us. "Especially not the Nile. Have you any idea how many lethal creatures live in the Nile? It's way too dangerous."

"Well, we can't stay here," Lux argues.

"She's right," I agree.

Edward rolls his eyes. "Big surprise," he says. "You agree with Lux."

I start to tell him where he can shove his big surprise when Lux gasps.

"Don't move!" she whispers.

"Why not?" Edward looks around.

"Don't—move!" Lux hisses.

I try to stay motionless yet still see what she's staring at, but that's pretty hard. So I slowly move to look over in the reeds—then I freeze. I stop breathing, and my heart starts to pound.

There in the reeds, only two baseball-bat lengths away, is a pair of black beady eyes staring at us. I can hear breathing. A snout pushes through the reeds. A chalk-white snout. It is a crocodile. A white crocodile watching us intently.

My mouth goes dry, and my legs tremble.

"What?" Edward whispers. "What is it?"

I lower my voice. "Just . . . don't . . . move."

Frustrated at being the only one who doesn't know what's going on, Edward turns around and sees the croc for himself. Then he faints. Just collapses into a heap on the sand.

"Fantastic," Lux mutters.

The white croc creeps forward through the reeds and slowly lumbers toward Edward. The thing is at least fifteen feet long, with muscular legs, black claws, and sharp yellow teeth. He pads silently toward us, his big belly as wide as a canoe and his brilliant liquid-black eyes staring right at us.

"What do we do?" I whisper.

"On the count of three," she says, "we run for the boat. You grab your backpack, and I'll get Edward. Got it?"

"Got it!"

"On your mark, get set, *go!*"

She dives for Edward, tossing him over her shoulder as if he were a sack of turnips in a tuxedo. She sprints for the boat. I watch in terror as she tosses Edward's unconscious body into the skiff and hurries to untie the rope.

"C'mon, AZ! C'mon!" she shouts frantically.

I look down at my feet. They're not moving.

I thought I was running right along with her, but I'm not. I'm planted right there on the beach. I look over, trembling. The crocodile suddenly lunges toward me. I shriek and bolt for

the water. Lux can only watch helplessly as she pushes the skiff off the beach and sticks an oar down into the shallow river bottom. She bobs there in the current and waits for me to jump in.

I shout loudly at the croc as I run. "CROCODILE PURSE! ALLIGATOR BOOTS! REPTILE FARM! SUSHI! SUSHI! SUSHI!" They are all the words I think might scare a crocodile.

I'm only a few feet from the skiff when I notice Lux frantically pointing and shouting.

"Backpack! Backpack!"

My yellow backpack!

I circle back quickly and grab it, leaping over the white crocodile's tail. The croc roars in anger and charges after me as I dash to the river. I slog into the warm water and try to reach the boat before the powerful jaws can snap shut around my legs. The water explodes behind me as the crocodile bursts toward us, bellowing so loudly his foul breath feels like a furnace blasting against the back of my neck.

I throw my yellow backpack into the skiff and lunge for the railing. I land half inside the boat and half out. Lux hauls my legs over the railing just as the giant white croc strikes and slams into the side of our boat like a freight train.

Lux starts to paddle like crazy and yells at me to grab the other oar. Dazed, I sit up and scramble for it. I quickly kneel in the bow of the skiff and sink my oar deep into the river, paddling for all I am worth. We gradually gain distance, and the croc sinks into the water, losing interest in the chase.

Time passes. An hour. Maybe two. I can't remember. All I know is it's starting to get dark and my arm muscles are burning. The river narrows, and the current slows down as dusk settles. Strange animal calls fill the air. Shrill shrieks and guttural growls echo from the jungle, which seems to rise up and close in all around us.

"Let's find a place to stop," Lux says.

Edward suddenly sits bolt upright. He starts shouting, "What are we doing in a *boat*? I told you I wouldn't get into a boat! How did we get here? Nobody gave you permission to put me on this boat!"

"Yeah?" I say. "Nobody gave *you* permission to faint!"

"This is kidnapping!" Edward snaps. "Kidnapping is a felony."

"Edward, just sit down," Lux says with a sigh.

But Edward won't listen. He tries to stand. Wobbling around, he almost capsizes us until Lux smacks him with an oar.

"Edward!" she yells. "Sit down!"

He sits down.

"You ought to be thanking us," I tell him. "If we'd left you back there, that huge croc would've had your tasty little English muffins with tea!"

Edward frowns at me. "So we escaped one croc. Do you have any idea how many creatures reside in the Nile that could easily kill us? We're going to die out here! This river is filled with man-eating crocodiles! Charging hippos! Flesh-ripping piranhas! And snakes—poisonous ones! There's the cobra, the black mamba, the green mamba, the puff adder, the horned viper, and the boomslang, to name a few!"

I smile sweetly at him. "Calm down, Edward. I have antivenom in my backpack."

"Oh, do you?" He sneers back at me. "Do you really? Unfortunately, if any of *those* snakes bite you, you won't need antivenom, AZ. You'll need a coffin!"

Lux sighs. "Edward, shut up already."

"There are also thousands of ways to get lost," he says.

I snort at him. "You mean *lost-er*?"

CHAPTER FOUR

"No. I mean that thousands of waterways connect and branch off this river. Tributaries that look just like the river, but they're not! They're dead ends that snake around for miles and flow into reedy swamps where there's no way out."

I glance at the wide, calmly moving river. "How the heck could we *lose* the Nile? It's like losing an airport runway."

"Well, airport runways are also highly dangerous."

"Jeez, Edward. What *don't* you worry about?"

"Not much," he answers glumly, looking into the water.

"All right," Lux says. "Look. We've got about an hour of light left. I haven't seen that croc for a few miles, so let's find a place to make camp somewhere on the bank. OK?"

We all agree and start to scan the riverbank for a safe landing place, which is not easy to find. The river's edge is tangled with overgrown jungle and thickets of tall reeds. Patches of lotuses float by, and blossoming trees close in around us.

As we look for a place to camp, Edward continues to treat us with an endless list of gruesome facts about the Nile.

It's the longest river in the world, he explains. It's home to the Nile crocodile, which weighs up to fifteen hundred pounds and can grow twenty feet long. They're responsible for approximately two hundred deaths every year. Officials have found quite a few interesting things inside crocodile bellies: human heads, airplane parts, cell phones that were still ringing, even smaller crocodiles!

And speaking of mummies, ancient Egyptians mummified crocodiles in the city of Crocodilopolis. There, everybody worshiped crocodiles and glued jewels to the crocs' heads. They believed the crocs were the sons of Sobek, the crocodile god.

Darkness begins to settle on the river, and birds fly low in the sky. We find a place to tie up the skiff—a shallow bend in the river where branches hang low like a canopy.

"You and Edward can go on and look for a spot to camp," I say. "I'll tie up the boat. I know how to tie every knot there is."

Lux smiles as she gives me the rope. My face feels hot. She's so pretty when she smiles.

Edward and Lux jump out of the boat. I tie it up tightly, then follow after them. We climb up the bank through scrub and stinging acacias. Looking for a place to make camp, we finally settle on a small clearing underneath a huge palm tree.

The three of us make a small fire and sit down for a minute. Only then do we finally realize just how damp, dirty, and hungry we are. We're *starving*. Thanks to that croc, we never had a chance to eat the food I'd collected and stashed from the jungle.

I pull out all the quick, edible-as-is snacks I'd found— the dates, mulberries, and lotus flowers. Then I remember the green gumdrops and tiny lamb chops in my pocket from the party back at the museum.

Lux gratefully snacks on the wintergreen gumdrops, but she refuses to touch the lamb. I forgot she doesn't eat meat.

"I don't eat anything with a face," she says. "Sorry, but frankly, I think those lamb chops are disgusting."

"Not to mention stolen," Edward says with a smirk.

"OK, want some grubs instead?" I reach into my backpack and pull out the jar filled with grubs wiggling around.

Edward reels back in revulsion.

Lux studies the jar, then frowns. "Hmm . . . I can't tell if they have faces."

"They're really nutritious!" I say.

"And I'm *really* not eating them," Edward replies.

"What about centipedes?" I pull out my centipede jar.

Lux squints at the jar. "Nope. I won't eat it. I can see faces."

Edward looks pale. "God save the queen," he says.

I shrug. "What's the big deal? What's common cuisine in one country can be an exotic edible in another. We don't eat insects in our culture, but other cultures do. Like in Korea, they eat steamed silkworms called *beondegi*. They're considered a delicacy."

"Revolting!" Edward says.

"Sick!" Lux says.

"C'mon, guys. Trying new food is the best way to experience other cultures."

Edward snorts. "Right. And it's the best way to experience projectile vomiting!"

Lux giggles.

I can't believe these two. I think *beondegi* sounds awesome. I'm going to add it to my BIG food list.

I drop a handful of wiggling white worms into my mouth and crunch down. "Fine. Suit yourselves. Will you guys eat fish at least?"

"I don't know," Edward says. "What kind of fish?"

"I won't eat it," Lux says. "Fish have faces, and I don't eat—"

"Anything with a face." I sigh. "Got it."

"I'll just eat the dates, mulberries, and lotus flowers," she says, quite content.

I decide to find some fish anyway, mostly because I'm still starving. I walk along the banks of the river. I know what I'm looking for—I saw it once on a nature program, and I've always wanted to taste it.

I find a muddy spot and start digging. This is *muddy mud*. Squishy and squirmy. I'm soon covered in the stuff. I look like the jungle floor. But I don't find what I'm looking for, so I pick

My B.I.G. Food List

What?	Where?	Notes?
*World's Biggest Sno-Cone	Lubbock, Texas	* The largest sno-cone ever made, it weighed 11.38 tons or 25,080 lbs. That's as heavy as 11 cars and a scooter stacked on top of each other!
* Space Station Astronaut Sticks	International Space Station	* Food that is specially processed into long, thin sticks so astronauts can fit them inside a special pocket on their helmets.
* Fugu	Japan	* Fugu is a poisonous puffer fish, filled with lethal tetrodotoxin. Only specially trained chefs can prepare the fish.
* Pizza Royale 007	England	* This pricey pizza costs $4,000. It has lobster, caviar, smoked salmon, venison, & edible 24-karat-gold flakes on it!
* Rocky Mountain Oysters	Colorado	* Fried bull testicles often served with cocktail sauce!

another spot. And then another. Each time, I dig a foot or so down into the slippery mud.

"Got it!" I finally shout.

The others come running to see what I've caught. A slithery, slimy thing is still wriggling in the mud. I wrestle it out of the ground, and everyone steps back. It's the ugliest fish you've ever seen. I use a rock and give it a quick, merciful death. Lux doesn't think it's quick *or* merciful, however. She stomps back to the campfire.

"That's a *fish*?" Edward asks, horrified. "Why isn't it in the water?"

"It lives in the mud."

"Whoever heard of catching a fish in the mud?"

"Me, luckily. It's a lungfish. When the river dries up, the lungfish buries itself in the mud for protection. It has primitive lungs, so it can live underground for a long time. It waits for the water to rise so it can get back to the river."

At last, it's my turn to be the know-it-all. I'm very proud of my exotic food intel. I just wish someone else was impressed by it too.

I roast the fish over a small campfire and serve it with some roasted fig chutney I had in my backpack. Edward just picks at the fish. Lux won't even look at it.

After eating our various dinners, we settle in by the campfire. I take the stereopticon out from my backpack and study it.

"Be careful with that," Edward says.

I roll my eyes. "I *am* being careful—" Just then, I drop it. "Oops! No problem! I got it!" I quickly retrieve the magic lantern and dust it off. "Good as new."

"AZ," Edward says with a sigh, "no offense, but I've seen algae that were smarter than you."

"I wonder what it's like to be algae," Lux says. "I mean, the Egyptians believed you could turn into any animal you wanted after you died. I wonder if anybody ever chose to become algae or a single-celled amoeba."

"I think lions and eagles were a little more popular," Edward says.

"I'd be a lion," I say. "Then I could eat everybody!"

"Shocking." Edward rolls his eyes.

"Fine. What would you be? A slug seems fitting."

"I'd be a cephalopod," he says.

I look at him. "A *what?*"

"Cephalopods are a class of animals that includes the octopus. The octopus is the smartest creature on earth besides humans," says Edward. "It has the ability to learn. It can open locks and escape almost any aquarium over time. Plus, it can open soda cans."

I shrug. "Big whoopee-ding."

"*Big whoopee-ding?*" he says. "*You* try to open a soda can with no thumbs."

"Any more of those gumdrops?" Lux asks.

I give her the rest of them. I keep only one for myself, saving it in case of an ultra-ultra emergency.

"So, what about you, Lux?" I ask. "What would you be?"

"Hmm. I think I'd be a scarlet macaw. They eat mostly fruits and nuts and can fly up to forty miles per hour!" she states. "Okay, how about this question: Which world explorer would you guys be?" she asks. "My favorite explorer is Amelia Earhart. She was the first female pilot to fly solo over the Atlantic Ocean. People said women couldn't fly airplanes, but she ignored them and did it anyway. She was a rebel. I got my pilot's license in honor of her."

I look over at her, impressed. "You have a pilot's license?"

"Airplanes are easy," she says. "Helicopters are harder. A lot harder."

"Yeah." I nod as if I know. "Anyway, my favorite explorer is Howard Carter. Everyone said the Valley of the Kings was completely explored and there was nothing left to discover. But he still searched that valley for over thirty years. Finally, he found King Tut's tomb! That's my kind of adventurer. There's also David Livingstone, who crossed the Kalahari and discovered a route from the Zambezi River to the coast of Africa. He also discovered most of the Nile."

"Isn't that the guy who got lost on the Nile?" Edward mutters. "For, like, five years?"

"Six years," Lux corrects.

"Well, it was an approximation," Edward says with a sniff, smoothing down his lapels.

Suddenly, I look around. "Guys, if a famous world explorer like David Livingstone can get lost for six years out here, what are the chances we'll ever get back home?"

We all just sit there. Nobody says anything.

At that moment, a low, bone-chilling growl comes from

depths of the jungle. We all look at each other, terrified.

"*What was that?*" Lux whispers.

"I don't know," I whisper back. "Maybe someone—or *something*—is watching us."

"Sounds like a large predator," Edward says matter-of-factly. "They just discovered a new species of Saharan cheetah that hunts at night and doesn't ever drink water. It gets all the liquid it needs from blood."

Lux and I glare at him.

We all agree to sleep in the boat for the night. That way, if we need to escape, we're already on the water, and that's the last place a Saharan cheetah can go. Probably. But we still have to worry about piranhas and crocodiles.

I suggest we sleep in shifts. While Lux and Edward try to settle in and get comfortable, I take the first watch. I listen to the strange sounds coming from the jungle, and I make notes in my adventure journal. I stay awake as long as I can. But then I let out a big yawn, and my eyelids get heavy. My head nods, and I fall into a deep sleep.

THE BLACK PYRAMID

Edward yells, "*Wake up! Wake up! Wake up!*" He starts smacking me with an oar.

"Ow!" I sit up. "What's your problem?"

Edward is furious. "My problem is that you fell asleep—and now we're here!"

I look around. I don't recognize anything. We're not under the low-hanging branch we tied the boat to last night, that's for sure. The wide river has disappeared. Now the boat bobs in a tall patch of raspy, marshy reeds. I can't see water anywhere.

I look over at Lux, who is scanning the area carefully. "AZ," she says, "do you have binoculars, by any chance?"

"Yep," I reply, digging into my backpack. "So, do you know where we are?" I ask her.

"Exactly where we shouldn't be!" Edward shouts. "Off the

main river, stuck in the mud!"

I rub my head. "We must have come untied during the night and the river carried us downstream."

"And who tied up the boat?" he demands.

"Well . . . I did. But it was . . . I mean . . ."

"Is there anything you don't destroy, wreck, or ruin?" he asks me. "I told you we shouldn't be in a boat! Now we're completely stuck! We can't get out. No one will ever find us! We're going to die out here, a million miles from civilization!"

"I wouldn't say that," Lux says, squinting through my silver binoculars. "Looks like civilization beat us here by a few millennia."

"What do you mean?" I ask.

She points behind me. Beyond the thick reeds is the top of a small black pyramid. At first, I think I'm dreaming. But I close my eyes and look again. It's still there—a black pyramid sitting on the bank of the Nile.

"Heavens," Edward says. "I think those are the black pyramids of Meroë."

"The black pyramids of what?"

"Meroë. It was a great Nubian city built by the Black Pharaohs. Nubia was an ancient kingdom with a blend of African and Egyptian culture."

"Maybe people are over there," Lux says. "Workers or archaeologists or even tourists!"

"Yes! And maybe they have snacks!" I stand up quickly, making the boat wobble. "Maybe they have camel kabobs!"

I jump overboard and land with a loud *ker-SPLOOSH* in the mud. It oozes up to my knees. Edward and Lux reluctantly follow me. We make our way to shore loudly, our feet going *slump-sludge-glerp-glop* in the thick mud.

CHAPTER FIVE

When we finally reach the shore, we climb up the bank to the first black pyramid. Behind it, we see another pyramid. Then another one and another one! It's a whole city of pyramids. Hundreds of them! They stretch from the thick brush out into the desert. We run giddily past the pyramids, shouting at each other and calling out for any signs of life.

But we find nothing. Nothing but silence. The black pyramids are all sealed shut. They are strange looking too. They're made of black stone and are not very tall.

We find an ancient cistern by the edge of the city, a circular stone well that catches fresh rainwater. Even though it was built in ancient times, it still works. We fill our canteens with stale but drinkable water.

That's when I notice a black pyramid nearby that isn't sealed. The entrance is open, like a gaping mouth set in the dark slate stone. I point it out to the others.

Lux quickly caps her canteen. "C'mon, guys. Let's check it out!"

"I'm not going in there," Edward says.

Lux sighs. "Why not?"

"Because exploring unknown archaeological sites without proper equipment and a support crew is unsafe, unsound, and directly against Alliance procedure."

Lux sighs. "Well, *we're* going in. Right, AZ?"

I nod slowly as I look over at the dark, menacing entrance of the pyramid.

"You don't want to go in there," Edward insists.

"Well, *you* don't want to stay out here," Lux snaps back.

"And why not?"

"See that cloud in the distance?"

We squint at the stretch of sand on the horizon. Just above it is a swiftly moving band of darkness.

"What is that?" I whisper.

"*That* is a sandstorm," she says. "It'll be here in about ten minutes. We'd better get a move on."

Edward sighs, and we all start jogging toward the pyramid. It's farther away than it seems. We keep looking over our shoulders to see the sandstorm quickly approaching. It's bearing down on us. We run faster and faster until we reach the doorway, then we collapse on the sandy floor. Our throats are sharp and burning from the dry heat, and our legs wobble like rubber.

Outside, the sandstorm hits the pyramid hard. I've never seen or heard anything like it. It rumbles and thunders and shrieks like a wild animal howling all around us. Long ribbons of sand start swirling in, lashing and licking at us from the doorway. We scamper back into the recesses of the dark antechamber and huddle in the corner, coughing and choking.

"What is in here?" Edward howls.

"I can't see!" shouts Lux.

That's when I remember my handy yellow backpack. I dig out a flare and light it, causing a burst of fiery orange sparks to shower down from my outstretched hand to the floor. In the flickering red-orangy glow of the flare, we see a narrow opening across the antechamber. The opening is just a slanted rectangle cut out of the wall.

We stay hunched over and shield our eyes from the stinging sand as we make our way toward the opening. It turns out to be the entrance to a long sloping tunnel. We don't even argue about whether to head down it. The howling sand drives us into the narrow tunnel. The ceilings are low, so we have to crouch and go single file.

It's the first pyramid I've ever been inside. I've dreamed

about this moment my whole life. But instead of feeling excited, I feel exhausted, scared, and hungry. I wish I were back home in my room, with Mom calling me downstairs for dinner. I'm starving.

Finally, the tunnel ends, delivering us into another large subterranean chamber. My flare is almost spent, so I light another one. Then I light two more, one for Edward and one for Lux.

We explore the room in silence. There's not a speck of grit or sand anywhere on the smooth black floor. It's damp and humid down here. The walls are made of massive black blocks of rock. Each must weigh over a ton. Yet every gargantuan stone is cut perfectly with laser precision. You couldn't even slide a credit card between them.

As we walk, the hairs on the back of my neck tingle. I can't help but turn around, expecting to see someone behind me. It's strange.

"I feel like someone's watching us," I whisper.

"Someone is," Edward says. He stops and holds his flare up higher to see.

I turn around and let out a big shriek. There, staring at us, is a giant sphinx carved out of black stone. It has the body of a lion and the head of a man. The head itself is as tall as a building.

"Well, we're definitely in Meroë," Edward says.

"How do you know?"

"Because that's a statue of Taharqa, one of the greatest pharaohs of the kingdom of Kush."

"Why does he have the body of a lion?"

"The ancient Nubians loved lions. They even had a lion temple, where their lions lived in luxury. The Nubians fed their enemies to them."

I look up and swallow.

Silence pours in around us. Again, I have the weird feeling we're being watched.

"Maybe we should go back," I whisper.

"Yes," Edward agrees. "Let's go back. We don't know if this place is structurally sound."

Lux scowls with disgust. "Edward, it's a pyramid. You know—those big stone triangle things that last for millennia? Do you really think it'll fall down today?"

Edward sniffs. "Well, statistically, it's not impossible."

We hear a distant thumping sound, and Lux leans in to listen. "The sandstorm is kicking up," she says. "I say we stay here until it passes."

CHAPTER FIVE

Edward reluctantly agrees.

As we make camp, Edward translates the hieroglyphs on the walls. "See here?" he says. "That's the crest of Meroë. They called Meroë 'the city of light.'"

He goes on to tell us Meroë was the ancient capital of Kush. The Nubians built some of the most amazing cities in the whole Egyptian empire, but they built them south of modern-day Egypt, in northeastern Africa. Meroë was their crowning jewel, one of the richest cities in the land.

He shows us a section of the wall with two maps carved into it. He points first to the map on top.

"This is a map of where we are right now. It has the crest of Meroë on it too. Here's the road where we came in. Here's the cistern where we filled our canteens. And here's the pyramid we're standing in right now."

Lux squints. "And the map beneath it?"

Edward shrugs. "I don't know exactly. It's a map of a completely different city. Different crest, different roads, different royal palace. According to the hieroglyphs, they call it 'the city of night.'" He traces his finger along the hieroglyphs from left to right. "It says, 'The city of light and the city of night dwell together here on one site. Together but separate, one in eternal sun and one in an eternal night.'"

"What does *that* mean?" I ask.

"No idea."

"Maybe the other city is underground?"

"No way," Edward says. "Look at the map. A city this big couldn't possibly be built underground. You couldn't ventilate it or get water to it. It would be impossible."

"Nothing is impossible," I tell him.

"Right." Edward rolls his eyes. "Except for things that are impossible, like an ancient metropolis being underground."

"What's that over there?" Lux holds up her flare and walks over to a large pile of wooden crates stacked in the corner. "Look at this, you guys. They're supplies left by some expedition team."

We investigate the crates, which are marked: FRAGILE and PERISHABLE.

"Hamburg Expedition," I read as I inspect the labels on the large wooden boxes.

"For your information, Hamburg is in Germany, which I assume you didn't know," Edward tells me, his nose in the air.

"For your information, I *did* know that!" I snap back. Of course I know where Hamburg is—it's the home of the hamburger!

Lux kicks one of the boxes open. It's filled with food rations and cooking supplies. We find tins of sugar, crackers, cornmeal, and corn syrup. The food inside is old but edible.

"Any mosquito repellent?" Edward asks, slapping his arm.

I pack up as many of the expedition supplies as I can, shoving the tins in my backpack. I hope to use them all in some spectacular vegetarian dinner Lux will remember for the rest of her life. But I'm not sure exactly what I can make with sugar, crackers, corn syrup, and . . . centipedes. Never mind. I'll figure it out.

Edward discovers a small leather journal inside one of the crates. The journal must have been left by one of the German expedition members. Pages of the journal are torn out, it's badly water stained in places, and the handwriting is hard to read. But we can still make out certain passages.

"This entry is dated April 1930," Edward says.

"We know the stereopticon transported us back to 1930," Lux states. "We don't know what month we're in. But I'm assuming that the German expedition was here not that long ago. Maybe they were here even a few weeks ago."

Edward nods. "Looks that way." He keeps reading. "It says the expedition found some sort of . . . entrance."

"Entrance to what?" I pipe up.

"To another city."

"A city?"

He nods. "It says the entrance is right here in this room."

"Where?" I look around but see nothing. "Does it say where?"

"I'm reading as fast as I can," he snaps. Then he adjusts his glasses and reads the last entry to us: "The expedition is getting tired. We've found the city of light, but still we have not unlocked the city of night . . ."

"What *is* the city of night?" Lux asks.

"No idea." Edward shrugs. "But it says the entrance is right here in this chamber."

"Where?" I say again, looking around one more time.

"It's hidden, idiot!"

"Oh."

He keeps reading. "The expedition must move on soon. We'll leave all our heavy supplies behind. If we're going to unlock the wand, we must find a key or a . . ." He pauses and tries to focus.

"A what?" Lux asks. "Find a what?"

"I can't read it. I can make out an *r*, but the rest is all smudged."

"Let me see." Lux takes the journal and studies it, frowning. I hold my flare up so she can see better.

"I can't read it either." She starts flipping through other pages. "Hey, did you see there are hieroglyphs in the back?" she says. She squints harder at them. "I know a bit about hieroglyphs, but these look kind of weird. Don't they, AZ?" She holds the journal out for me to see.

I nod—as if I have any idea what's on the page. It all just looks like crazy scribbles to me.

"The symbols look strange because they're not Egyptian," Edward says. "They're Meroitic." He walks back to the lion statue, running his hands along the glyphs carved into the black stone.

I hold my flare higher to see. "Mer-*what*-ick?"

"*Meroitic*—the language of Meroë."

"I remember now," Lux says, nodding. "Their language was different from all the other traditional Egyptian hieroglyphs."

"I briefly studied Meroitic hieroglyphs at the museum," Edward says. "It was during an exhibition of Nubian goldsmithing. Their work was amazing."

"That's great, but what did it mean by 'unlock the wand'?" I ask him. "Is it like a magical wand?"

Edward's flare fizzles out, and I light him another one. He looks up at the massive stone statue. "I wonder if it could mean the Wand of Horus."

"What's the Wand of Horus?" I ask.

"Nobody knows exactly, but almost every statue of an ancient Egyptian pharaoh or god has one. And look, Taharqa has one too!" Edward excitedly points up to a short cylindrical object in the ancient pharaoh's right hand. "That's a Wand of Horus! Some say they were just shorter versions of a royal staff. But others think the wands had special properties. Maybe they were filled with some metal alloy that conducted energy and gave the pharaohs longer life."

I look over at Lux. "Think that wand could somehow open the entrance?" I ask her.

"Let's find out," she says with a grin. "Quick—give me another flare."

I hand her a new flare, and to my surprise, she clamps it between her teeth. Then with the still-burning flare in her mouth, she quickly scales the statue to the lion's paw. Amazing.

She holds the flare up to the wand and shouts down at us, "I think I found something!"

"What?" I shout back.

"On the end of the wand, there's an indentation . . . like a keyhole!"

"A keyhole?"

"It's rounder than a keyhole. It's a weird octagon shape. Hang on—I'm coming down."

She jumps down to the floor. Removing the flare from her mouth, she grabs her canteen, taking a swig from it.

"What do you think it can be?" she breathlessly asks us.

"I don't know," Edward says. "To unlock the entrance, the journal says they need a key—or something that starts with r."

"So, what starts with the letter r and could open a door?" Lux ponders.

I shrug. "A ratchet? A racket? A rattle? Or a rock? Or a ring?"

"What?" She looks over at me.

"What?" I repeat.

"You said a ring."

"Well, I'm just thinking out loud."

"AZ, *what about the ring on your finger?*"

I look down. "You think the Alliance ring could open the Wand of Horus?"

She nods.

"That's mad," Edward says.

"Why? It's an octagon, isn't it?" she replies. "And we know it's an ancient design."

I slowly take the ring off my finger, handing it to her carefully. "Try it," I whisper. "Try it and see."

With the flare back between her teeth, she quickly scales back up the statue and sets the ring inside the Wand of Horus.

"It fits perfectly!" she shouts down.

"Turn it!" I shout back.

She does. A moment later, we hear a deep rumbling sound. The whole room seems to shake. Lux jumps down before she's knocked off. She hits the ground just in time—a second later, the giant statue of Taharqa shudders. Dust spills from the seams above. Then the massive statue splits in half and rolls open like a huge grinding set of automatic doors at a grocery store.

Once the entrance is completely open, we stand there, frozen in place. We just stare.

We're too shocked to make a sound.

THE LOST CITY OF SECRETS

My heart hammering, I stand there before the open statue. I slowly start to make sense of the image before me. It's a doorway, an entrance to a huge marble hall filled with tall gold pillars and colorfully painted murals.

Lux looks down in shock at the ring still in her palm. As if in slow motion, she hands it back to me. I carefully wedge it back on my thumb. Not losing this now.

We all peer into the chamber, using our flares to reveal what is in front of us. At the far end of the room is an archway with a symbol—a large symbol.

"Is that what I think it is?" Lux whispers.

"It can't be," Edward answers.

I squint as I look up. "Isn't that the symbol we saw back

at the museum? The symbol for that city Heinrich found. The symbol for . . ."

"*Ophir!*" Lux says.

"No!" Edward shakes his head. "It *can't* be!" he repeats.

Lux begins to smile. "But, Edward, it is! It's the symbol for Ophir!"

She's right. It's exactly like the symbol stamped on the pottery shard back at the museum. A crooked arrow inside a circle—I'd remember it anywhere.

"Does that mean this is Ophir?" I ask them.

"There's only one way to tell," Lux whispers.

"It's not Ophir!" Edward crosses his arms. "Preposterous!"

"Fine. You stay here, Edward." Lux looks at me instead. "Let's go check it out!"

I nod, and we begin to walk through the lion's mouth and into the grand hall.

"Wait a second!" Edward calls after us. "It could be dangerous. It could be a trap!"

"Edward," Lux says, looking over her shoulder at him. "If this is what I think it is, then we've discovered one of the greatest archaeological finds ever. We'll be famous!"

At that, Edward smiles too. "They'll write about us in history books!" he adds.

"All right, then," Lux says. "Let's get our stuff and go explore!"

We step into the grand hall and look around. The whole space is glowing with a warm, rosy light.

"Why is it so bright in here?" Lux asks, peering into the hall. "It should be dark, like the other chambers."

"Up there." Edward points. "I think those are quartz crystals. See the glowing stones in the recesses above the pillars?"

"How can they be glowing?" Lux asks.

Edward takes off his glasses and polishes them. "I read about solar-powered quartz crystals in ancient Egypt," he says. "Quartz can conduct electricity. Radios had quartz crystals in them when they were first manufactured. So these crystals must be connected to a solar-powered energy source somewhere up above ground."

I roll my eyes and start walking toward the archway. Edward is such a know-it-all.

We cross the marble entrance hall to the archway. We

stand there for a moment, peering down a dark road that seems to spiral into the earth. The road is made of dull dark-green stone.

Edward kneels down to touch it. "Ophir's Royal Road!" he whispers. "I've heard legends about this. It's cut from one solid piece of emerald."

I look down. "This road is solid emerald? But it's not polished and shiny."

"Indeed," says Edward. "This is how emerald looks in its natural state."

Lux starts walking, but she gets only a few steps away before Edward pipes up.

"Should we really go down there?" he asks. "Is it safe? I mean, what if we get trapped?"

"Edward, this road probably leads to the lost city of Ophir. We *have* to go down there. As Amelia Earhart would say, the goal is worth the risks. Stop worrying!" says Lux.

"Yeah, Edward," I say. "Stop worrying."

"Besides," Lux says. "Remember the Ruby Tablet? If it's down here somewhere, we have to find it before anyone else does."

She has a point. When I first heard about the Ruby Tablet, I assumed it was just a legend. Yet here we are—standing on what sure seems to be the Royal Road of Ophir. If the Ruby Tablet is actually real too, then it's one of the most powerful artifacts on earth. Uncle Arthur said it has the recipe for making gold!

We head down the road, with Lux leading. Our steps are heavy in the silence. It's so quiet, it's as if the place were surrounded by a glass dome.

"OK," Lux says after a while. "So where would they keep the Ruby Tablet?"

"Somewhere safe," Edward says. "Somewhere secure."

"Like a vault?" I offer. "Or maybe a temple?"

Lux nods. "We'll have to search everywhere."

As we walk, we see that the city is built inside a series of underground canyons, vast cathedrals of empty space. The Royal Road twists and spirals like an elegant green corkscrew, winding down through different levels of the city.

An underground city—looks like Mr. Know-It-All was finally wrong about something.

We pass through a complex system of roads and buildings. There are whole neighborhoods with hundreds of dwellings carved right into the rock, like honeycombs. We walk through wealthy neighborhoods with elegant marble mansions and beautiful gardens paved with mosaic courtyards. We also find working-class neighborhoods with smaller mud-and-brick houses and narrower streets.

"People lived down here?" Lux says. "But how did they get water?"

We soon find out. We see cisterns, wells, drainage channels, public fountains, and private baths.

"Amazing," Edward says. "This water is pouring down into the city from the Nile. They must have cut channels into the bedrock and made tunnels and reservoirs down through the rock to divert water from the river. Ophir had as much water as anyone could need!"

As we wander farther down the road, we see parks, temples, and carved obelisks, which look like mini versions of the Washington Monument. There's also a large white marble building with pillars. Edward tells us it's called *the house of life*. It was an ancient Egyptian learning center—part school and part scriptorium. A scriptorium is a school and a library rolled into one. Scribes there documented old books and kept records of everything from funerals to weddings to magical spells to the chief physician's medical procedures.

"We might find something about the Ruby Tablet in the house of life," Edward suggests.

We walk up the wide stone steps and head inside. The tall walls are lined with jasper, a bloodred quartz. The deep stone shelves hold thousands and thousands of ancient Egyptian "books." They don't look like regular books, though. Some of them are carved on stone slabs and clay tablets. Others are painted on wooden boards.

Most of them, though, are written on thin rolls of parchment called *papyrus*, the reed we saw at the river's edge. Edward says the Egyptians liked to use papyrus because it was lightweight and easy to handle, transport, and store. It was also cheaper to make than most alternatives. Unfortunately, it was also less permanent. It survived only under special circumstances.

"That's why this is incredible!" Edward says with a gasp. "There are more papyrus rolls here than I've ever seen before!"

The "books" are all neatly organized by subject matter on the shelves. We carefully search for anything about the Ruby Tablet. That is, Edward searches. Lux has a basic understanding of Egyptian hieroglyphs, but not of Meroitic. And I can't read hieroglyphs at all, though it is a skill I intend to acquire the minute I get home. Well, the first thing I'll do is eat my weight in delicious home-cooked food. Then I'll take a long, hot three-hour shower and sleep for a week. After that, I'll learn hieroglyphs. Probably.

Edward looks and looks, but none of the books is about the Ruby Tablet. He frowns.

"Maybe the Ruby Tablet really is a myth," Lux says with disappointment.

"Or maybe it isn't," I tell her. "Maybe it's just a really well-

CHAPTER SIX

kept secret. I mean, if I had the recipe to make gold, I sure wouldn't stick it in the local public library."

"AZ's right," Edward says. "They'd keep the tablet's location a secret."

"What?" I exclaim. "Did you just say I'm *right?*"

"I'm already regretting it," Edward groans.

We leave the library and continue walking down the Royal Road, which is now a wide boulevard. After a while, we come to a towering, ornate palace. We head inside and search it completely: the reception halls, the dining pavilion, the kitchens, the royal bedchambers. Every square inch is covered in paintings, carvings, and treasures, but we find nothing.

"We're definitely coming back here to make camp tonight," Lux says, gazing up at the tall marble pillars.

Back outside, we come across a large open-air marketplace filled with stalls that still contain ancient wares. We find leather sandals and white linen tunics, alabaster jars of perfume, woven rugs, incense burners, jewelry, furniture, and papyrus-reed baskets. We even find a stand selling clay animals and little toy boats carved from wood. Lux finds a rag doll stuffed with papyrus and cotton. And Edward finds an ancient board game carved on a slab of wood with colorful glass marbles.

I find a row of food stalls. Ancient Ophirians ate vegetables, fish, meat, fresh bread, sycamore fruit, and honey-drizzled figs. We also pass bakeries and butcher shops. Some stalls are still filled with big burlap sacks containing spices: sea salt, black pepper, ground cumin, sesame seeds, and dried dill.

We continue on to find stalls selling glass jars, cosmetic boxes, and two-handled vases called *amphorae*. There are ancient wigs with musty stiff black hair and short black bangs chopped bluntly. I try one wig on, admiring it in an ancient silver mirror. I'm just messing around. But Edward—as always—

has to turn it into a "teachable moment."

He explains that both men and women wore makeup in ancient Egypt. They made green eye paint from copper and made black eyeliner, or kohl, from lead. Creams and oils were used like sunscreen protecting the Egyptians from the hot desert sun.

"Not much hot desert sun down here," Lux points out.

"True, but they believed makeup had magical healing powers as well," Edward says.

"Good enough for me!" I say. I take a crumbly piece of a kohl pencil and draw two big fake eyebrows on my forehead.

Edward sighs, but Lux giggles, so it's worth it.

We make our way down to the second level, which is more industrial. We pass workshops that seem to belong to artisans. Images are carved in the stone walls of each workshop: weavers making rugs, physicians mixing medicines, stonecutters carving coffins, perfumers pressing flowers, and metalsmiths polishing intricate crowns.

"Ophirians were trained to become excellent at their particular trade," Edward says. "The bread bakers baked the best-tasting bread. The tomb painters painted the most beautiful tombs. The embalmers prepared the most well-preserved mummies."

We pass painting studios with large stone pestles for grinding colors. We see pottery workshops with enormous stone kilns. Row after row of pottery wheels all sit motionless, and tall terra-cotta vases are lined up like clay soldiers. The stone sculptor's workshop has long wooden tables with metal chisels laid out and blocks of marble and limestone. The furniture workshop has tools hanging on the walls. We recognize hammers, chisels, and mechanical drills. Large cedar shelves are filled with painted chests and ivory-inlaid chairs.

In the jeweler's workshop, much finer tools hang above wooden workbenches, where we see unfinished pieces of gold and silver jewelry. In the cobbler's shop, we see animal skins stretched out on a rack to dry. Pieces of leather have been cut and are ready to be stitched into shoes.

The cosmetic workshop looks like an ancient laboratory, with long stone counters and shelves of stone jars and amphorae. The perfumery has large sacks of dusty flower petals. We find sacks of orris root, cardamom, myrrh, and cassia. The wig shop has strips of linen pinned neatly to wooden mannequin heads.

We finally come to a shop filled with lutes, harps, lyres, horns, and other instruments.

"Think they still work?" Lux wonders.

"Only one way to find out!" I grab a horn from the shelf

and blow, emitting a loud groaning sound into the cavernous space. We have a parade right there in the street—me blowing on a brass trumpet, Edward whistling into a silver flute, and Lux banging on a drum. Shouting and singing, we make a considerable racket as our sloppy parade marches down the empty boulevard. We hail ourselves the new kings and queen of Ophir. We practically fall down laughing.

Suddenly, Lux says, "Look!" She points down to the bottom level of the city, the ground floor.

We peer down with her.

"Great Scott!" Edward gasps.

There below us is a huge, beautiful pink lake. We leave our instruments and run down the Royal Road to the bottom level. We're now miles underground.

Around the lake, we discover a sprawling industrial center with wide streets and supply warehouses. We see textile mills, buildings for fermenting barley for beer, loading docks, brickyards, smelting shops, pigment factories, chariot factories, stone quarries, gold mines, silver mines, iron mines, and clay pits.

We also find a huge underground arsenal of weapons, mostly for the city's battalion of archers. Edward informs us that Ophir had world-renowned archers in their army. The Ophirian army was so strong that by 1000 BCE, they won their independence from Egyptian rule. Several centuries later, they then seized control of the empire, and the great Nubian king Piye became the pharaoh of all Egypt.

Every building is connected by a network of man-made canals that artfully crisscross the city. They all meet in the center at the massive pink lake. We walk around the lake. Submerged lights make the water a warm, rosy pink. On one end is a gushing waterfall that pours down the canyon wall. We

find a large port with long docks and a giant hoist to lift cargo on and off ships.

"I don't get it," Lux says. "Why would they build these big boats? They're five miles underground. They're way too big to get up the Royal Road. And why is there a hoist to load them with supplies?"

Nobody knows.

"What's that?" I point to a stately gray granite building.

"That's a *wabet*," Edward says. "An ancient Egyptian funeral parlor. That's where they prepared the mummies. Behind it is the wabet temple."

"No way!" I turn around. "An ancient Egyptian funeral parlor? Can we go in?"

Together, we cautiously walk into the wabet, which is a large L-shaped building. The short side of the L is the high priest's temple. It's locked up tight. The long side of the building is the embalmers' work area. It's a large room filled with empty stone tables and lots of scary instruments: saws, knives, scalpels, and more.

I point at a tray of instruments. "That's the same brain-scooping hook we saw in the museum, isn't it?"

Edward nods. "Indeed, it is. As I described back at the museum, they used that long metal hook to pull out the brain through the nose. They pulled it out chunk by chunk and scooped out leftover bits with a spoon."

Lux looks green. "Don't remind me!"

"They didn't keep brains?" I ask. "I thought they saved organs for the afterlife."

"Not the brain," Edward says. "They didn't think they'd need a brain on the other side. I mean, look at you, AZ—you don't even need one on this side!"

"Funny." I shoot him a look.

"Sorry." He smirks. "Anyway, after the brain was out, they removed all the abdominal organs except for the kidneys—they didn't think they were important."

"I love kidney bean pie!" I shout. I'm really hungry.

Edward says the embalmers always left the heart in the body. They believed the soul lived there. The rest of the organs were coated in cedarwood resin, wrapped in linen strips, and sealed inside terra-cotta pots called *canopic jars*. They washed out the chest cavity with palm wine and stuffed it with straw. The body was covered with natron salt and left to dry out for over a month.

Once the body had dried, it needed purification. Priests performed rituals on the body, and embalmers repacked it with perfumed linen. Then they sewed it up and wrapped it in almost *a mile* of long linen strips.

Once the mummy was wrapped, they put it in a *suhet*, a coffin painted to resemble the person inside. Then it went to the tomb and was sealed inside.

I glance around the room, trying to imagine the mummification process taking place. Then something on the ground catches my eye.

"Hey!" I point down. "What's that?"

"A priest's mask," Edward says. "It's meant to represent the jackal-headed god of death, Anubis."

I hoist up the heavy terra-cotta mask of Anubis. It looks like an evil jackal.

"Priests really wore this?" I ask.

"They were the overseers of mysteries and wore that mask when purifying the dead."

I stick the mask on my head. "OooOOOooo!" I croon in my best spooky voice. "I am the overseer of mysteries!"

But when I try to take it back off, I can't. The mask is

stuck on my head.

"Uh, a little help here?" I ask Lux through the mask.

With a laugh, she helps me yank it off.

The first thing I see is Edward shaking his head. "That's it—I'm reporting both of you for abuse of antiquities."

The second thing I see is the city lights getting dimmer. The water of the pink lake fades to dark rose.

"Hey!" Lux says. "What's happening to the lights?"

"They must be solar powered," Edward guesses. "As the sun goes down and the light fades up there, it'll fade down here too. I'd say we have about fifteen minutes before it's dark."

I look around the huge space. "How dark?"

"Well, unless the Ophirians hung a moon in here, I'd say completely pitch-black."

We look at each other, then start running. There's no time to lose—we have to reach the royal palace to make camp.

Once we reach the royal palace, Edward and I drop our gear in the main hall. Out in the courtyard, Lux builds a fire on the floor. She uses old linen, a stainless-steel camping fork from my backpack, and her Tecpatl knife as flint. I'm repeatedly impressed by her.

Starving, I prowl around until I find the palace kitchen. It's filled with wooden racks still holding large storage jars, cooking vessels, and bowls. With the ingredients in my pockets, I make a filling meal of dried figs and lotus flowers. This meal tastes even better than yesterday's. It's true that hunger is the best sauce.

Lux smiles at me. "AZ, you could make a meal anywhere from anything!"

"Well, it's easy when you've memorized so many recipes," I tell her.

It's true. I've come up with many of my own special recipes

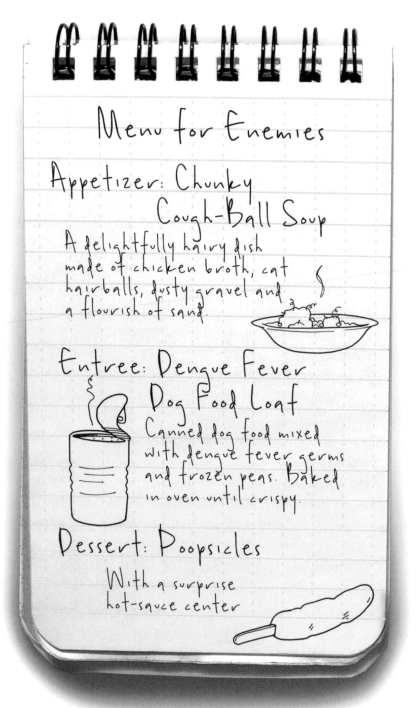

Menu for Enemies

Appetizer: Chunky
Cough-Ball Soup

A delightfully hairy dish
made of chicken broth, cat
hairballs, dusty gravel and
a flourish of sand.

Entree: Dengue Fever
Dog Food Loaf

Canned dog food mixed
with dengue fever germs
and frozen peas. Baked
in oven until crispy.

Dessert: Poopsicles

With a surprise
hot-sauce center

and menus. I even have one for enemies.

After dinner, we sit around the crackling fire.

"We need to figure out what we can do tomorrow to find the Ruby Tablet," Edward says.

"Yes, but that's just the beginning," Lux says. "The real question is, what will we do if we actually find it? What if we find the recipe to make gold?"

I know what I would do.

The others have their own ideas, of course.

"I'd buy an island and make it an international animal sanctuary," Lux says.

"I'd build a museum," Edward says with a sigh.

"I'd just make a bunch of gold," I tell them.

"And then what?" Edward asks.

"I don't know. Hide it in my house?"

"AZ, you're a moron."

"At least I don't want to build some dumb museum!"

Lux changes the topic. "Do you think we're cursed because we entered the lost city of Ophir?"

Edward laughs. "There's no such thing as a curse."

I look at him. "Are you kidding me? Of course curses exist. The ancient Egyptians invented curses. The first dude who opened King Tut's tomb got bitten by a mosquito and died a month later."

Edward rolls his eyes. "Lord Carnarvon is the 'dude' you're speaking of. And he died from pneumonia, not a silly curse. There's no such thing."

"OK, then answer me this: Why and how was a mosquito inside a sealed tomb? Huh? It has to be an undead mosquito! A zombie mosquito!"

Edward sighs at me. "You know, it's really a pity you haven't gotten help."

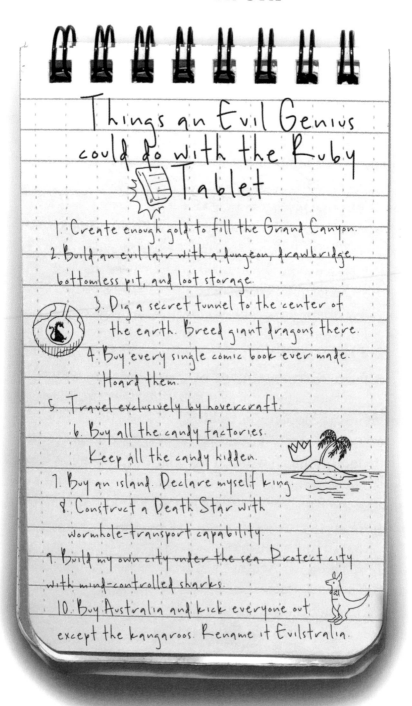

Things an Evil Genius could do with the Ruby Tablet

1. Create enough gold to fill the Grand Canyon.
2. Build an evil lair with a dungeon, drawbridge, bottomless pit, and loot storage.
3. Dig a secret tunnel to the center of the earth. Breed giant dragons there.
4. Buy every single comic book ever made. Hoard them.
5. Travel exclusively by hovercraft.
6. Buy all the candy factories. Keep all the candy hidden.
7. Buy an island. Declare myself king.
8. Construct a Death Star with wormhole-transport capability.
9. Build my own city under the sea. Protect city with mind-controlled sharks.
10. Buy Australia and kick everyone out except the kangaroos. Rename it Evilstralia.

"A zombie mosquito?" Lux smiles. "I'd actually like to see that, a tiny bandaged bug flying around."

"Do you believe in the afterlife?" I ask them.

"I believe that when you die, you go to another place," says Lux. "Somewhere far away, and you see everyone you've ever known who's died. Friends, family members, even pets."

"So, heaven has hamsters now?" Edward says. "Brilliant."

"Maybe. I don't know," Lux says. "I just think we all see one another again somehow."

"How perfectly . . . *unscientific*," he says. "And ridiculous."

"Well, the ancient Egyptians sure thought they were going somewhere!" I say, defending Lux. "They put everything from furniture to toothbrushes in their tombs. Why else go to all that trouble preserving their bodies and doing those complicated rituals?"

Edward stares at me. Actually, he stares through me. He's deep in thought.

"Rituals . . . rituals . . ." he mumbles slowly. Suddenly, he breaks into a grin. "Of course! Why didn't I think of it?"

"Think of what?" Lux asks.

"Rituals! The high priest! He controlled the most sacred manuscripts and the inner sanctum. It might be a lead for the Ruby Tablet!"

"What's the inner sanctum?" I ask.

"That's where Egyptians kept their most valuable treasures," he says. "Most cities had one in a temple some-where."

"Okay. So where would this inner sanctum be?" Lux asks him.

"I'm not sure, but the high priest's altar in the wabet temple is the place to look for clues. Remember that part of the wabet building that was locked? That might be it."

"Well, what are we waiting for?" Lux jumps up. "Let's go look right now!"

"Right now?" Edward frowns. "But it's dark."

"So?" counters Lux.

"So, it might be dangerous," he says.

Lux refuses to back down. "What do you think is out there? An army of earthworms?"

"I think Edward's right," I say reluctantly. I don't particularly want to back Edward up, but I definitely don't want to go creeping around out there at night.

"You guys are big babies." Lux flops back down on the floor. "You're scared of everything."

"Maybe," Edward says. "And maybe you aren't scared of *enough*. Charging around without thinking isn't always the best way. Sometimes you have to plan things out."

"I like taking action," Lux says.

"I've noticed," I tell her.

"Well, it beats waiting around here all day," she says with a shrug.

"We're not waiting all day," Edward says, staring into the crackling fire. "We're waiting *for* day. There's a difference. Right now, I suggest we try to get some sleep, so we're fresh in the morning. Then we can strategize with clear heads and hash out a plan."

Once again, I agree with Edward. Reluctantly.

CHAPTER SEVEN

TRIED, TRUE, AND TESTED

In the morning, I make pancakes using a tin of expedition cornmeal, another tin of powdered milk, and some dehydrated butter. I season the batter with cinnamon from my backpack. First, I cook up some pancakes for Lux. Then I toss some leftover centipedes into the remaining batter. Centipede Pancakes. It's a classic. Warm, filling, and high in protein—not to mention excellently crunchy. I like crunchy. (Of course, I keep this secret ingredient from Edward.)

After breakfast, we set off for the wabet temple. We know it's locked, so we look for another way in. But there are no other doors, no windows, and no other entrance of any kind.

"How do we get inside?" I ask Lux.

"Maybe we could knock a wall down," she wonders.

Edward gasps. "Absolutely not," he says with a sniff.

CHAPTER SEVEN

"There will be no deliberate destruction of ancient artifacts on my watch!"

Lux groans and stomps off. A minute later, she returns. "I think I found another way inside the temple," she says, "but you won't like it."

She leads us into the main section of the wabet and stops in front of a square hole in the wall.

"I think we can get into the temple through here," she says.

"What is that?" I ask.

"It's a mummy tunnel," Edward says. He nods, clearly understanding what Lux has in mind. "You're right. This will work."

I don't understand, though. "What's a mummy tunnel?" I ask.

"They used this tunnel to send prepared bodies from the wabet to the temple for blessing," Edward explains.

"Seriously?" I look at the square hole and frown. "A mummy tunnel?"

"It should take us right into the temple," he says. He then frowns. "Do you think you'll fit? Because . . . you know . . ." He gestures toward my midsection.

"Yep," I say confidently. "No problem."

I know I can crawl through that square hole. It's about the same size as the hole the lunch-tray conveyer belt comes in and out of at my school's cafeteria. And I've crawled through that loads of times. I even served two weeks' worth of detention to prove it.

"Come on, guys," Lux says, crawling in. "Amelia Earhart said the best way to do something is just to do it!" She disappears into the tunnel.

Edward and I look at each other and quickly follow her.

Tried, True, and Tested

We crawl single file in the pitchdark, feeling along with our hands as cobwebs tickle our faces. The tunnel is definitely a squeeze. At any moment, I expect us to bump into an overweight mummy who got stuck in here centuries ago.

Finally, we reach the other side. Lux helps pull us out.

"This is definitely the high priest's chamber," she says, gazing about the room. "Look at that altar."

"High *priestess*," Edward corrects. "That's the royal symbol for Amenirdis."

"Am-and-who?" I look at him.

"I remember now—Ophir had a high priestess, not a priest," he says. "Her name was Amenirdis. She was a powerful Kushite princess and the sister of the great Kushite pharaoh Piye."

"A high priestess? I love this city!" shouts Lux.

"Well, now what do we do?" I ask, looking around the temple.

"Let's check over here," Edward says.

He leads us up onto the altar. There, we see a large stone dial in the wall. It's big—the size of a tractor tire. It's covered in carvings of some kind.

"I think what we're looking for is behind here," he says.

"What is that?" I ask, pointing at the dial.

"It's a cipher wheel."

"Oh yes." I nod as if I knew what he's talking about. "I thought so."

"What's a cipher wheel?" Lux asks me.

My face immediately goes red. "What is it? Um . . . it's a . . . kind of . . . uh . . ."

For once, I'm relieved when Edward interrupts.

"A cipher wheel is a kind of puzzle—an interlocking one that opens something up once you've solved it. It's like the combination lock on a school locker."

"So what does this one open?" she asks.

"Not sure," Edward says, shrugging. "There might be a room behind it or even a tunnel."

"A tunnel to where?" Lux asks.

"Only one way to find out," he says.

He moves closer to study the wheel, and we follow. Now we can see that the stone disc is actually several stone discs. They each rotate separately. As Edward explains, the goal of unlocking a cipher wheel is to line up all the rings correctly by matching all their symbols together.

It sounds easy enough, except I don't recognize a single symbol.

How can anyone know if the snaky squiggle goes with the two-headed triangle? Or if the upside-down trapezoid belongs with the semicircle holding a pitchfork? The whole thing looks harder than a math test crossed with a science exam stuck before a track meet on a day when you had to skip lunch.

Edward, however, is not stumped. "I'll solve this in ten minutes," he boasts. "Tops."

"I'll solve it in one!" Lux replies. "I bet this thing is so old, it'll just crack open!"

With that, she kicks the cipher wheel with her foot.

"No!" Edward shouts. "Don't! They're rigged for intruders!"

We all freeze as the cipher wheel shudders slightly. Breathlessly, we wait a moment and look around. Nothing happens.

"You can't mistreat the mechanisms," he whispers. "They'll lock permanently if someone tries to destroy them."

Lux shrugs. "Well, it looks like this one isn't rigged."

Just then, we hear a sound. It seems to be coming from a nearby statue. I step back as the statue's mouth opens, revealing a dark hole. Lux and I both see it, but Edward doesn't. He's too focused on the cipher wheel again.

"All right," he says, mostly to himself. "The symbols on the outermost ring are animals. We have a crocodile, a lion, a scorpion . . ." He looks at the second ring. "And this one is covered with Egyptian gods . . ." He grins. "So simple! You just line up the animals with the gods they represent. Let's start with you, Mr. Sobek. You go with the crocodile. Now, for Thoth and Hathor . . ."

Meanwhile, Lux and I hear a series of clicks.

Clickita-clickita-clickita!

"What was that?" Lux asks.

"It came from in there." I point at the statue, trying to peer inside the hole without getting too close.

"Edward?" she asks as calmly as she can. "How long did you say it would take?"

"Not very long now," he says.

Clickita-clickita-clickita!

"Lux!"

I point at another statue. Its mouth is open too, and something black and sparkly is coming from it. Soon, the face is completely covered with a shiny black beard that appears to be moving.

"Beetles!" Lux shouts. "Beetles are pouring out of the statues!"

Suddenly, all the statues in the room are swarming with big black scarabs. A pool of large clicking beetles boils upward and outward across the floor.

"Now, for the fourth ring!" Edward says, still oblivious to the beetles.

"Hurry, Edward!"

"The fourth ring is . . ." He frowns and steps back, mindlessly crunching on a beetle. "They're not deities or planets." he says. "Hmm . . ."

Clickita-clickita-clickita!

Now a thick river of beetles swarms in from the statues. The beetles spread out like an oily carpet on the floor. Lux and I jump on nearby pillars as Edward continues to solve the puzzle.

"Could they be symbols for the pharaoh's sons and daughters?" Edward mutters.

"Edward!" Lux shouts. "Hurry! Before we're beetle juice!"

The tide of black scarab beetles roils and rises higher. *Clickita-clickita-clickita!*

Edward stares blankly at the cipher wheel. He's stumped. Meanwhile, the beetles keep coming, wave after wave. A bleak resignation falls over me. We are dead.

"We can't die," I say desperately. "I haven't even tasted albino white gold caviar yet! It's supposed to be delicious. It's a thousand bucks a spoonful!"

"What?" Lux gapes at me. "Why in the world are you thinking about *gold* caviar right now?"

"Gold . . ." Edward whispers, still staring at the wheel. Then he suddenly lets out a whoop. "That's what the symbols are! Precious metals! Gold, silver, copper—metals the alchemists used to make!"

"Edward!" Lux shouts. "Less talking, more dialing!"

Edward looks over his shoulder. For the first time, he registers what's going on behind him. His eyes go wide, and he flies to the wheel, spinning the symbols as fast as he can.

"Just one more!" Edward shouts. "Just one more!"

"Hurry!"

Clickita-clickita-clickita!

"Got it!" Edward shouts as the final symbol locks into place. "It's unlocked!" He pushes on the wheel, but it won't budge. "Help me! I can't open it—it's too heavy!"

Lux and I leap over the moving mass of beetles. The three of us put our shoulders into the massive stone wheel. Still, it won't move.

"Are you sure it's unlocked?" Lux shouts at Edward.

"Yes! I heard it—"

Just then, the wheel gives way, opening like a door. We all tumble through, falling headfirst down into a raging torrent of water.

We're swept away on some kind of crazy stone waterslide that swoops and plunges, twists and turns. It shoots us down faster and faster until one by one we land in

a frothing cauldron of churning water. *Kersploosh! Kersploosh! Kersploosh!* The water is cold, and a strong undertow pulls at our legs.

I sputter and choke, struggling to stay above the rough waves, but it's no use. I feel the water pulling me under. My body is so tired, and my brain is so boiled. I go limp and close my eyes.

Suddenly, Lux surfaces and shouts at us. "I think I found a way out underwater!"

"Underwater?" Edward croaks.

She nods. "It looks like the entrance to an underwater tunnel."

I frown at her, fighting to stay afloat. "How long is it?"

"Don't know."

"How long would we have to hold our breath?"

"Don't know."

"Sounds too risky!"

"Much too risky!" Edward shouts. "We could die down there!"

"But there's no other way out!" she yells.

We frantically scan the steep, slick walls of the cauldron. She's right. There is no other way out, and the water is rising all around us.

Lux goes first. She takes a big breath and dives underwater. I follow with Edward clinging to my backpack. We swim down into the opening of a tunnel.

Lit by an eerie yellow light, the tunnel is covered with an ornate, colorful mosaic depicting Egyptian gods and mythical creatures. The tiles and jewels sparkle in the dim green water. It would be beautiful—if swimming through it wasn't so terrifying. We swim and swim, pulling ourselves along the tunnel with our hands. The tunnel twists and turns, getting wider and then narrower at different points.

At last, I see the end. I kick with all my strength, my lungs bursting, my eyes burning, the light all around me growing dim.

I think I might be drowning.

Suddenly, a great force pulls us forward, and we burst out of the tunnel and into the light. Gasping for air, we fall back into another raging torrent, tumble over a massive waterfall, then *splash!* We're underwater again.

THE EYE OF HORUS

J ust as my lungs are about to explode, I burst onto the surface of the water. I gasp and gulp for air, my heart pounding. The strong current pulls me into a churning whirlpool at the bottom of the waterfall. I'm trapped. I look around for the others.

"Edward!" I sputter as I thrash wildly. "Lux!"

I see Edward hoisting himself onto the bank of the indigo lake. Lux is already onshore and helping to pull him up. I swim hard in their direction and stagger out of the raging water, choking and gasping. We lie on the bank, trying to catch our breath. I look up at the arched ceiling above us. It's smooth and polished and made of luminous white stone.

After a few minutes, I manage to sit up. We're sitting beside another necropolis, a network of honeycombed tombs carved into the rock wall behind us. The necropolis is flanked by lakes. On one side is the indigo lake we just climbed out of. It's rough and turbulent. And on the other side is a sea-green lake. Its surface is as smooth and polished as stone.

In the center of the lake is a white pyramid that looks like an iceberg floating on the water. A long white walkway runs from the shore, out across the lake to the pyramid's tall silver doors.

It's warm down here. My shirt is soggy, and I wring it out in sections, squeezing as much water as I can.

"Which way should we go next?" I ask.

"That way," Lux says, nodding at the white pyramid in the middle of the sea-green water.

"What is it?" I ask her.

"Maybe the entrance to the inner sanctum," she says.

"Probably not," Edward replies. "Getting here was too easy."

"That was *easy?*" It makes me cough and sputter again.

Edward nods. "What I mean is, we're not done yet. To find treasures, heroes almost always go through three tests. The tests are meant to determine if you're worthy enough to find the treasure."

"So, the tests keep the riffraff out?" I offer.

He smirks a bit. "Yes. That's one way to put it. Anyway, I believe there are three tests to pass before entering the inner sanctum. And we just passed two of the tests without even realizing it. We passed the test of intelligence by solving the cipher wheel and the test of bravery by swimming through the tunnel and going over the falls. But I bet there's one more test up ahead."

The three of us look out at the ominous white pyramid floating in the lake. We're silent for a moment as Edward's words sink in. Wow, we've passed two tests already. Without even realizing it! We're real explorers—real heroes! "Worthy" enough to pass the tests! I swell with pride for a moment.

But then I sigh. Technically, Edward and Lux passed the tests. Edward was intelligent enough to figure out the cipher wheel, and Lux was brave enough to lead us through the underwater tunnel. Me, I seem to just be a tagalong. Maybe I'm the riffraff the tests are trying to keep out.

Lux notices my long face. "AZ, we're a team," she says gently, as if she can read my mind. "We're in this together, helping each other at every step. Just think—Edward wouldn't have been able to solve the cipher wheel if you hadn't mentioned that gold caviar."

Edward nods—somewhat begrudgingly—to acknowledge this is true.

"And maybe I was the one who said we should go through the tunnel, yet we each had to do it. We each had to be brave enough to swim all that way and risk our lives." She smiles. "So let's work together to figure out this next test."

I smile back at her, feeling a little better. Even Edward has to smile.

"Okay," I say. "So what's next?"

"I don't know," Edward says. "Let's go find out."

We collect our things and set out across the long narrow walkway. I'm nervous as we cross over the lake. I half expect piranhas to start leaping out of the water at us, but nothing happens. The only sounds are our footsteps on the walkway and the waterfall fading behind us. Still, it feels as if we were being watched.

We finally reach the white pyramid. On the tall silver doors, there's a carved picture of the jackal-headed god holding a large golden scale. Beneath him is a line of hieroglyphs.

"That's Anubis," he reminds us. "Like the masks in the wabet." He then studies the hieroglyphs. "Only the worthy may

enter," he translates.

Carved into the white stone above the silver doors, a large eye stares down at us.

"That's the Eye of Horus," Edward says. "It's a symbol of protection."

"Well, let's hope he protects us," Lux says.

She reaches out to open the silver doors, only to discover that they can't be opened. We have no clue about how to open them. They have no doorknobs, hinges, or handles. We stand there on the pyramid's stone platform and stare at the doors.

"Now what?" Lux asks.

"No idea," Edward says with a sigh.

He takes off his glasses and leans against the pyramid as he starts polishing them. Suddenly, we hear a grinding sound. Then a stone panel slides opens—it's small, about the size of a cereal box. We see a small alcove with a little shelf cut right into the stone.

We peer inside. Sitting there is a brilliant gem about the size of a baseball.

"Whoa!" I whisper. "What's that?"

"A diamond," Edward says, leaning closer.

"But it's huge!"

Edward reaches out for the diamond, but I grab his arm.

"Don't!" I whisper. "Bet it's booby-trapped."

Edward quickly yanks his hand back and nods. We all stare at the diamond, unsure what to do next.

Then Lux gazes at the carving above the door. "Edward," she says, "why is Anubis carrying a scale?"

"Those are the scales of judgment," he says. "Ancient Egyptians believed that when you died, you went to the hall of justice and your heart was weighed on a scale against the feather of Maat. If you had been a good, honest person in life, then your heart was as light as the feather, and you were allowed to enter the kingdom of Osiris."

"And what if your heart *wasn't* as light as a feather?" Lux asks.

"Then your heart was devoured by Ammit, a monster who was part hippopotamus, part lion, part crocodile. Without a heart, you couldn't move on to the other side. Instead, you had to wander in oblivion for an eternity."

"Sounds like my math class," I say.

Then I get an idea.

"Hey, wait a minute! This is the third test! Like you said, Edward, we've already passed two tests: the test of intelligence, when you figured out the cipher wheel, and then the test of bravery, when Lux led us over the falls. The door says, 'Only the worthy may enter,' which means someone who's wise, brave, and . . . honest! That's it! We have to be honest—we have to not take the diamond!"

"Not steal the diamond?" Lux looks at the sparkling jewel. "How do we 'not steal' the diamond? Stand here for a while? Just leave it in the door and don't do anything?"

"No," I say, shaking my head. "There must be something to *do*. The hero always has to do something to pass a test."

"Like what?"

I think for a moment. "Let's try walking away—leaving the diamond behind."

Edward and Lux nod excitedly, thinking that might just work.

But when we turn around, we're shocked that the long walkway across the lake has disappeared. Gone without a trace. Once the panel opened, the walkway must've submerged underwater, and we were too busy to even see it.

"Great! Now what are we supposed to do?" Edward says. "Swim back?"

I break into a huge smile. "That's it! We have to prove we're honest by giving the diamond *back*."

"Who do we give it back to? And how, when we can't open the door?" Lux asks me.

"There must be a place to put it," I mutter. I step back and scan the face of the pyramid. "There!" I point to the Eye of Horus. "The eye socket! It's empty! I bet we're supposed to put it in there!"

Edward smiles too. "You might just be right, AZ! Let's give it a try."

We crowd around the alcove. I wipe my hands on my shorts and take a deep breath. Slowly, I put my hand inside the stone opening, expecting it to be chopped off at any second. At last, I grasp the diamond. It's smooth and cool to the touch.

"Got it!" I tell them.

The Eye of Horus is high above us, so I need a boost. Lux

quickly kneels down and clasps her hands together. I step on her clasped hands while Edward steadies my legs.

"Be careful!" he says. "Don't drop that diamond! It's priceless!"

"Gee, thanks," I say. "I had no idea."

Lux struggles to support me as I stretch my arm as high as it will go. I reach and reach and try to stick the diamond into the empty eye socket. Just as I almost have it in place, the jewel slips from my fingers and falls to the ground.

"No!" I shout, jumping down.

We stare in horror as the diamond bounces right off the platform and into the water. But then Lux plunges into the lake after it. Edward and I hold our breath as she disappears under the water.

After what feels like a long moment later, she bobs back up to the surface, grinning. The diamond is in her hand. She climbs onto the platform, dripping water.

"Heads up!" she says and tosses the diamond to me.

"Way to go!" I grin. "Nice diving!"

"All in a day's work," she says, wringing water out of her dress.

"Quite dangerous, though," Edward adds with a sniff.

She exhales loudly. "You're welcome, Edward."

Once again, Lux kneels down, and I climb onto her clasped hands. She wobbles as I reach up again with Edward doing his best to steady us all. This time, I finally manage to click the diamond into the eye socket.

I hop down, feeling about as awesome as I've ever felt before.

"Look!" Lux says. "The walkway is rising again."

I turn to see the long white walkway reappearing, rising slowly from the sea-green water.

"Well, that's a relief," she adds. "Now we can eventually

get back!"

As we gaze at the walkway, we hear a sound behind us. We turn back around to see the tall silver doors of the pyramid swinging open.

"It looks like we've been deemed worthy," Edward says.

Inside the white pyramid is a beautiful room completely tiled in mosaics of rich purple. At the center of the room is a white marble ramp, leading underground.

"The inner sanctum must be down there," Lux whispers. "Under the lake."

We're silent as we pass through the doors and head down the ramp. Along the walls are painted murals and hieroglyphs. When we reach the bottom, there's a set of tall gold doors embossed with a large winged creature.

"Edward," Lux says, stopping. "What's that on the door?"

"That would be a sphinx," Edward says.

"Right, but why would there be a sphinx on the door?"

Edward reads the hieroglyphs on the door. "The hieroglyphs indicate a sphinx is guarding the city."

Lux looks at him with wide

eyes. "A sphinx is guarding the city?"

"That's what it says," he replies matter-of-factly. "What's the big deal?"

Lux takes a step back. "Don't you know what a *sphinx* is?" she asks him.

"Let me see," Edward says. "Do I know about the ancient mythical creature that has the head of a human and the body of a lion, who guards sacred spaces and has a nasty habit of killing people that don't answer its riddles correctly? Yes, I know what a sphinx is."

"Exactly. A sphinx kills people!"

Edward raises an eyebrow. "You think there's a *real* sphinx in there?"

"Why else would there be a sphinx on the door?" Lux says. "It's like a 'Beware of Sphinx' sign!"

Edward turns to me. "And do *you* think there's a real sphinx in there, AZ?"

I shrug and shake my head. "I don't know what to think anymore."

"Oh, for heaven's sake!" Edward says. "You both read too many comic books. The sphinx is a legend created to deter tomb raiders—common criminals. Not scientists and explorers."

"Well, I don't care what anybody thinks," Lux says. "We're *not* going in there. We can't face a sphinx alone."

"And yet," a voice behind her says, "you will have to."

We whirl around to see a long shadow come down the ramp. A figure emerges, holding a gun.

THE RUBY TABLET

L ux finally says, "*Heinrich Schliemann?*"

I do a double take. It *is* Heinrich, the weird German archaeologist guy from the British Museum.

Another shadow appears behind him. It's his giant wife, Greta. A mean-looking white crocodile is waddling beside her on a leash. I swear, the croc somehow looks familiar. I stare at them with my jaw open. The picture is too strange for my tired brain to process. My software is jammed.

"Thank heaven!" Edward says, walking toward them with his arms extended. He seems to think Heinrich and Greta are some kind of rescue party. "How did you find us all the way down here?" he marvels. "Is my grandfather with you?"

"Edward!" Lux whispers at him. "He has a gun! People who are rescuing you rarely point a gun at you!"

"Oh," Edward says with surprise and disappointment. "I see." He clears his throat. "In that case, I feel I should mention that my grandfather can pay any amount of ransom. Well, for *me*, anyway."

Heinrich smacks his forehead. "What in zee world? I don't want a *ransom*, you stupid little turnip!"

Suddenly, Lux bolts, making a desperate attempt to reach the ramp. But Greta cuts her off, her massive, lumpy body blocking the way. Greta's pale face looks even meaner than it did in the museum. Her tiny black eyes are fixed on Lux. The crocodile beside her hisses. Lux slowly makes her way back toward Edward and me.

Heinrich chuckles. "My friend Pickle here would like

you to stay," he says. "I think he likes you! He was very much looking forward to seeing you again."

We all snap our heads to look more closely at the croc. Could it be? Is that the same croc that forced us into the boat and chased us downriver when we first arrived?

Heinrich grins at us. "That's right, my little scorpions! Pickle here has been very helpful. I must say, zee plan has gone perfectly since I brought you here!"

"Wait—*you* brought us here?" I ask, raising an eyebrow.

"Yes, my little swamp toad! Who else?"

"*You?*" Lux repeats.

Heinrich grunts in disgust. "Why are children so stupid?" he asks, turning to Greta. "Why they don't walk off a cliff every day of their lives is a mystery to me. It really is." Shaking his head, he turns back to us. "Yes, my little lunch meats! I brought you back in time to Egypt. Me, Uncle Heinrich!"

We glance at one another sideways, exchanging looks of disbelief. Is it true? Did Heinrich somehow transport us in space and time? The same ferret-faced man with the horrible haircut and weird-shaped head that we'd met at the museum? Before, he'd worn a bad suit. Now, he wears a bad safari helmet and a really bad, overly snug khaki jumpsuit covered with pockets and cropped at the knee.

"Only a *genius* could have pulled off such a complex scheme such as this!" Heinrich continues.

With that, I burst out laughing. I know it's not a good idea to laugh at someone pointing a gun at you, but I can't help it.

"You? A genius?" I cackle.

Lux and Edward cast me sideways glares. Obviously, they don't think laughing is a good idea either.

Heinrich's face goes red. "Yes!" he shouts. "I am a genius! Turns out your grandfather's 'secret room' is not so secret. Stealing a key was all too easy. I left zee magic stereopticon for you to find. I knew *you* would pick it up." He points right at me.

My laughter comes to an abrupt end. "The gumdrops," I whisper, feeling my cheeks turn pink. "You planted the green gumdrops next to the stereopticon."

It's Heinrich's turn to laugh. "One look at that chubby belly, and I knew you would go right for zee gumdrops, Snack Boy! And then I knew you couldn't resist zee stereopticon right next to them."

My cheeks burn hot.

With that, he pulls a flat wooden thing out of his vest pocket. He quickly snaps it into shape. It looks a lot like our stereopticon, only his must be collapsible.

"That's impossible!" Edward exclaims in shock. "How can you have a stereopticon too?"

Heinrich sighs and looks heavenward. "There is more than one magic stereopticon, you simple-minded slug."

"Really? How many of them are there?" Edward asks.

"Silence!" Heinrich shouts.

"Enough about the stereopticons," Lux says firmly. "Why did you bring us here, Heinrich?"

Suddenly, it all becomes clear to me. "I know why," I say.

"Oh, really?" Heinrich crosses his arms over his chest, smirking. "You know why? Well, then, please tell me, my little infected mosquito bite!"

I take a deep breath and look at Edward and Lux. "Heinrich lied about finding Ophir on the island of Cyprus,"

I tell them. "He knew the Lost City of Secrets was here under Meroë. But he couldn't get inside the city because he couldn't get past the statue of Taharqa. He needed an Alliance ring. He tried to join the Alliance, but they turned him down. So, he decided using someone else's ring would be easier than getting his own."

I look down at Uncle Arthur's ring and sigh. "Did I get that right, Heinrich?"

"Yes," Heinrich sneers. "When I saw a portly little boy with an Alliance ring, I knew what to do! You fell right into my trap with zee gumdrops. Actually," he says, "you fell into *all* my traps like zee good little blobfishes you are! When I sent Pickle after you, you ran right into zee boat I placed in zee reeds. And remember that growl you heard from zee jungle?" He makes a scary face, then laughs. "Me again! If I must say, I do a very good cheetah impression. You ran right back to zee boat, just as planned. Then once you little warthogs fell asleep, we dragged zee boat right to that marsh near zee black pyramids of Meroë. You certainly are heavy sleepers."

My breath quickens as I listen to Heinrich detail every single step that led us here. He's right. We did fall into his traps. It was eerily convenient that there was a boat waiting for us.

"I will say, though," he adds, "I'm quite impressed with your abilities, my little toadstools. You not only unlocked Ophir but also found zee inner sanctum for me!"

He claps his hands together. Greta smiles evilly. Even the crocodile seems to have an evil grin.

Heinrich licks his lips. "I would have killed you by now, but you are too useful. Your next task is to go inside those doors and answer zee sphinx's riddle. If you don't answer correctly, then she will kill you, and I will find someone else to send inside. On zee other hand, if you do answer her riddle and bring me zee Ruby Tablet, I will let you live."

"No you won't!" I shout.

"This is true," he says, sighing. "I will kill you. But I will let you live long enough to see me become zee most powerful man with zee most powerful artifact on earth!"

"No deal," I say angrily.

"Very well," he says and shrugs. "Then I will kill zee girl now."

Greta seizes Lux with her meaty fist and pushes her to the ground, right in front of the huge white crocodile. Lux shrinks back, looking terrified.

"No!" I shout. "Edward and I will go. We'll go . . . and we'll bring you the Ruby Tablet."

"Don't do it! No!" Lux screams. "Don't give it to—"

Greta's massive hand covers Lux's mouth, cutting her off. Lux struggles and squirms, but Greta has her pinned.

I look Lux right in the eyes. I know why she doesn't want us to get the Ruby Tablet for Heinrich. But I hope she knows why we have no choice. We can't let anything happen to her.

"I said, we'll bring you the tablet," I repeat, still looking at Lux. "But on one condition—you promise not to hurt her."

Heinrich shrugs. "Yes, fine. *Whatever.* You children are so boring—I want to stick a fork in my eye! Now go and get me zee tablet. You have until tomorrow morning. If you are not back here with zee Ruby Tablet by then, I will feed your little friend Lux to Pickle . . . and his friends."

"Pickle has friends?" Edward says, his face looking paler than usual.

Heinrich nods. "Many."

"We'll return by tomorrow morning," I say. "Come on, Edward."

Edward and I turn around to head down the ramp, but Heinrich stops us. "One more thing," he says.

"What?" I say as we turn around once again.

"Zee ring, please."

I glance down quickly at my Alliance ring. I shake my head at him. "I can't give you this ring."

"Why not?"

"Because I might need it . . . to open something. Like how we used it to open the entrance to Ophir. I'd better take it with me, right?"

Heinrich narrows his eyes. "Fine," he finally says. "You can take zee ring with you. But if you try anything funny, you'll pay, my little rotten avocado. You'll pay dearly. I'll take zee ring—and zee finger it is on!"

I nod quickly and tug Edward's sleeve. We turn around to look at Lux one last time. Even though she's pinned by a huge woman, being held at gunpoint, and inches away from a crocodile, the expression on her face suggests that Edward and I are the ones in greater danger.

"Ready?" I whisper to Edward as we walk slowly down the ramp.

"No." He shakes his head. "Absolutely not."

"Me neither," I confess.

With that, we step inside the sphinx's mysterious chamber, leaving Lux behind.

Possibly forever.

We find ourselves in a decadent domed chamber covered floor to ceiling with deep-blue glazed tiles. In the center of the room is an elaborate raised platform that serves as an altar area. Sitting on the altar is a huge statue of a golden sphinx. It has the body of a giant cat, the wings of a majestic bird, and the face of a beautiful lady. Propped on the animal's head is a gleaming Egyptian headdress. Other than the statue, the room is empty.

I step cautiously forward. "Hello?" I whisper. "Anybody here?" Nothing but heavy silence surrounds us.

"See?" Edward says, slapping my back so hard I stumble. "No sphinx! No roaming mummies or reawakened curses either! Just artifacts waiting to be discovered by those brave enough to find them!"

We warily cross the blue-tiled room. My eyes switch back and forth, waiting for something to pounce out at us, but nothing happens. We reach the other side of the room safely, arriving at another set of gold doors.

"Ready to see something amazing?" Edward asks as he pushes the doors open.

We see nothing. Just darkness. A heavy curtain is draped across the entryway.

"Terrific," I whisper.

Reaching out, Edward pulls back the curtain. Dust and debris rain down on us. Coughing, I look up—and freeze. We're standing at the doorway of the inner sanctum. A tall marble wall flanked by twin obelisks stands before us.

We race up a short flight of steps into an open courtyard with a mosaic tile floor and a large stone fountain. Beyond the courtyard is a river with a bridge arching over it. We cross the bridge and step into a grand hall lined with large columns. It's dark except for the light coming in through small windows cut near the ceiling. It's like walking through a forest of giant stone trees.

At the end of the hall, we find a vaulted room filled with gold columns and murals of gods and goddesses. In the center of the room is a sacred fountain surrounded by a circular pool made of solid gold. It's filled with shimmering golden water.

Gold light reflects up from the water and down from the ceiling.

Standing at the far end of the hall are two enormous golden statues: one of Apedemak, Ophir's favorite lion god, and the other of Isis, the Egyptian goddess of magic. Both statues have burnished gold skin that gleams in the light and headdresses that sparkle with thousands of jewels. Isis's eyes are twinkling diamonds, and Apedemak has glowing green eyes made from giant emeralds.

I bet each one is worth eighty trillion dollars.

Between the two statues is a long white marble hallway lined with tall columns. In between the columns are entryways to different rooms.

We search every room, looking for the Ruby Tablet. One room is a large auditorium filled with silver benches. Other rooms are lecture halls with lessons still scribbled on the slate walls. We also find a long hall housing thousands of ancient papyrus scrolls. Edward says it's called *the hall of eternal secrets*.

There's a study room filled with tables and chairs. Edward says these were for the inner sanctum scribes. They must have spent a lot of time down here, because we also find sleeping quarters, an elegant dining room, and a large kitchen still stocked with supplies.

We come upon a map room with all its walls covered in murals. There's a map of ancient Egypt and the world according to the Nubians. And on the ceiling, there's a complex replica of the night sky with the heavenly bodies and astronomical signs carefully illuminated.

Edward pauses in front of one of the maps.

"So that's how they got here!" he says.

"How *who* got *where?*" I ask. "What are you talking about?"

"Look," says Edward. "This is a map of Ophir's trade routes. The Bible says King Solomon's fleet started their

CHAPTER NINE

journey to Ophir here, at the northern end of the Red Sea." He
points to the spot on the map. "That's why everyone's always
looked south for Ophir—it was the only direction boats could
sail. To the east is Saudi Arabia; to the west, Africa; and to the
north, Egypt."

I nod, though I'm not really interested in a geography
lesson. Seconds are ticking away as we stand here.

"But see this blue line on the map?" Edward continues,
now pointing to the line. "It's an ancient canal. The hieroglyphs
say it was built by Ramses II, and it goes all the way from the
Red Sea to the Mediterranean Sea. We thought the two seas
had never been connected before 1869, when the Suez Canal
was built. But the Suez wasn't the first canal! According
to this, King Solomon sailed north from the Red Sea to the
Mediterranean through the ancient canal. He then pulled a
U-turn and sailed south along the Nile to reach Ophir!"

"That's cool, Edward, but we need to hurry."

"That's why King Solomon needed the Phoenician navy
to travel with him!" he says, pressing on. "Not because he was
crossing the Red Sea but because he was sailing down the
dangerous Nile! They would've had to navigate rapids and
carry the ship around waterfalls and through jungles—"

"Edward!" I snap. "Let's go! The tablet? Lux? Remember?"

Edward sheepishly tears himself away from the map,
and we move on. We search through chambers filled with
mysteries—unknown alphabets and strange mathematical
equations. One chamber has a doorway in the middle of it
and nothing else. The doorway is made of thick blocks of pink
crystal. We walk through it several times, but nothing happens.

We find huge laboratories filled with equipment and
experiments. One chamber has twelve thrones inside, each cut
from a solid crystal. Another room is made of solid silver, with

a large crystal orb sitting on a marble podium in the center. It all tantalizes our imaginations, but there's no time to figure out any of these mysteries. We need to find the Ruby Tablet.

Near the end of the marble hallway, I walk through one of the last doorways. Right away, every hair on the back of my neck stands up. I'm staring at piles and mountains of gold. Gold coins, gold amulets, and gold ankhs.

I pick up an ankh and study it. An elaborate cross, the ankh is the Egyptian symbol for life. This ankh has the symbol for Meroë on one side and the symbol for Ophir on the other. I put it in my pocket, concrete proof that the two cities are connected. Not that I'll live to tell anyone about it. Beyond the gold are mountains of emeralds, rubies, diamonds, and sapphires, all piled up like gravel.

The sight is so amazing that I almost miss a small doorway off to the side of the room. I assume it leads to a storage room filled with shovels for all the piles of gold and gems out there.

It isn't a storage room.

We step through the doorway into a small beehive-shaped room made of solid ruby. The floor, the ceiling, the walls are all ruby. The room glows crimson, like warm blood. In the center of the room is a thick slab of scarlet-red glass the size of a sled. It shimmers under the glowing quartz lights and pulses like a human heart.

It's the Ruby Tablet. We've found it.

"It looks like a big cherry-flavored hard candy," I whisper.

Edward nods.

The tablet is carved with tiny hieroglyphs. Once again, Edward studies it.

"It's true. This is the actual recipe for making gold," he says. "You can make enough gold to fill a bathtub! A swimming pool! An entire ocean!"

I'm speechless.

"What's more," he says, "the tablet includes directions on conjuring diamonds and rubies out of the earth. You can call them, just like a snake charmer calls snakes."

Remembering our mission, I snap back to life. "All right. Let's get this back to Heinrich before something happens to Lux."

"How should we carry it?" Edward asks. "What if it breaks?"

We find a silver cart with wheels in the jewel room. We line it with as much muslin as we can find. The fabric should hopefully keep the tablet from chipping or breaking. Then we turn to the tablet.

"Ready?" I ask him.

"Ready," Edward says.

"OK. Be careful. This thing could shatter. Here we go. One, two, three . . . lift!"

We lift the tablet off the gold stand.

Then we drop it.

For a second, we're dead silent. Then the shouting starts.

"*What did you do?*" Edward practically shrieks.

"*Me?* What did *you* do? I told you to be careful!"

"I was careful! But you—you're such a klutz! Look at what you did!"

Edward points down at the Ruby Tablet . . . which, amazingly, isn't even chipped. We both exhale with relief. Ruby is stronger than it looks.

We finally load the tablet into the silver cart. Just then, I get a weird feeling in my stomach. Suddenly, my mother's words echo in my head: A *true archaeologist cares more about protecting treasures than about finding them. . . . A relic is safe when it's buried; the true danger is above ground.*

I look at Edward. "We can't give the tablet to Heinrich," I say. "We can't."

Edward shakes his head. "I don't want to hand over the Ruby Tablet either, AZ. But what else can we do? It's the only way he'll free Lux."

"Yeah, but then he'll destroy the entire world."

And that's when it hits me. I remember the contents of my backpack.

"I have an idea," I declare.

Edward cringes. "Oh, I hate it when you say that."

I plunk my bright-yellow backpack on the table. "I think I have everything we need right here. And if we hurry, we just might pull it off in time."

"What are you talking about? What are we doing?"

I smile at him. "If Heinrich wants a recipe, let's give him a recipe!"

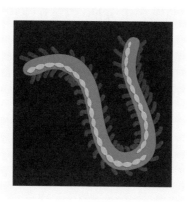

CHAPTER TEN

DOOMED AND ENTOMBED

We work all night and into the morning. After examining our hard work, we carefully lift the Ruby Tablet up from the worktable, wrap it in a large piece of cream-colored muslin, and load it onto the silver cart. The last thing we need is for this sucker to crack. We then navigate the cart around the sacred fountain in the golden reception room and through the forest of columns.

When we reach the golden doors of the sphinx's blue chamber, we decide it's best to back the cart into the room. We argue a bit about who will hold which door. As we stand there bickering with our backs to the chamber, I become aware of the sound of breathing. Not my breathing or Edward's. There's someone—or something—in the room.

"Did you just hear something?" I whisper.

"Like what?"

We slowly turn around. Immediately, I see that the altar is empty. The statue of the sphinx is gone.

Just then, a shadow moves in the corner. "*Hello, children,*" a voice purrs.

Edward and I look at each other and freeze.

My heart is beating quickly, and Edward swallows so hard I can hear it. We turn around to see the statue of the sphinx alive and staring at us.

"*Good morning.*" Her voice is as lovely as it is ferocious. It sounds like a melody of three voices singing together. It's a beautiful, rich, wonderful sound that makes all the hair on the back of my neck stand up.

Suddenly, the large feline animal pounces out from the corner and lands gracefully on top of the gold altar.

"*Welcome back,*" she says. "*I've been waiting for you.*"

Terror races into my hammering heart. My mouth goes dry. I hide my eyes, daring only to peek at the creature's enormous clawed feet. Then I gaze up at her muscular haunches to her silky mane and thick, sumptuous pelt that frames her beautiful, serene face. She has deep-black eyes like pools of oil. She is lovely—and horrible. We nearly die from the shock of it.

The sphinx moves as if she is suspended in water, springing from the altar onto the blue tiles, padding on her enormous feet.

"*It's an honor to defend the city,*" she says. "*Today I defend it against you.*"

Edward clears his throat. "No need to defend the city from us!" he stammers. "We're here to help! We're explorers, you know!"

"*Yessss,*" she hisses. "*We know.*"

CHAPTER TEN

We? Our eyes dart around the chamber, expecting to see some other creatures pop out.

"We didn't think you were real," I whisper. "You were just a statue when we came through here before."

"*True,*" she purrs, her tail switching. "*All may enter; few may leave.*"

As scared as I am, I remember Lux—her life depending on us. "So, you have a riddle for us?" I ask the sphinx.

"*True, true, true.*"

"And if we answer the riddle correctly, you'll let us through?"

"*We will. We will. We will.*"

I hesitate. "And if we get the riddle wrong, you'll . . . um . . ."

"*Devour you in the bowels of sweet hell,*" she purrs sweetly. "*You must die out of respect to the great sphinx. However, if you answer the riddle correctly, then I shall die, out of respect for you.*"

"Oh, that's really not necessary," Edward says. "A thank-you note would be fine!"

"Edward!" I hiss.

"*Be warned, travelers,*" the sphinx purrs. "*We have guarded the city for six thousand centuries. We do not lose often.*"

"So," Edward chuckles awkwardly, "not new to the job, then?"

"*Be cheered,*" she says. "*For if you answer my riddle correctly, not only shall you live but you shall witness a great sight, as well. Whenever a sphinx dies, the place she guards comes back to life for a single day, so all her citizens may honor her. Yesss, yesss, yesss. Now, are you ready?*"

We don't say anything.

Then the sphinx gives us a riddle: "*What rises with the river, flourishes with the sun, and then dies when the moon comes up?*"

We stand there frozen while her rhythmic tail switches back and forth.

CHAPTER TEN

Back and forth. Back and forth.

A voice says, "Is the answer . . . the kingdom of Egypt?"

I look at Edward, amazed at his response. But actually, he's looking at *me*. It takes me a moment to realize *I* was the one who had answered. I had said it!

The sphinx looks at me, and I shuffle nervously.

"Oh, did I say that out loud?" I cough. My cheeks turn red. "Pardon me, Your Sphinxiness. I didn't mean to say, um, anything."

"*He who begins the answer,*" she says, "*must finish the answer.*"

"We're doomed!" Edward says, pacing and frantically shaking his head.

I feel like passing out. I have to answer? *Me?* The one who failed both middle school math *and* gym class? Can I summon the answer from some unsuspecting treasure chest of knowledge I have buried deep inside?

Well, maybe I can. Something inside me came up with the kingdom of Egypt as the answer—without my even realizing it. Wherever that response came from, maybe there is more.

I clear my throat. "The kingdom of Egypt rises with the river," I begin slowly, "because the Nile floods the desert every year and feeds the crops. Egypt also flourishes with the sun. The ancient Egyptians worshiped the sun gods Horus, Aten, and Ra. Their civilization began to die when the Assyrians attacked, carrying the image of a moon and star on their shields. After that, Egypt fell into decline. Eventually, it became part of the Roman Empire. The Egyptian sun gods were replaced by Roman deities, astrological symbols that could be seen only in the stars, up in the night sky."

Whoa.

I look around the room. Where the heck did that come from? The sphinx bows down low to me. "*You have spoken with wisdom*," she says. "*You have given the correct answer.*"

"What?" Edward gasps. "No way! Are you sure?"

"Shut up, Edward!" I say, glaring at him.

"*I now must leave the city,*" the sphinx says, "*and begin my journey to the other world.*"

"Are you . . . are you going to die?" I whisper.

"*I am, I am, I am,*" the sphinx sings.

I feel really sad. I turn away a little, so Edward can't see that I have tears in my eyes. I want to ask the magnificent creature more questions, but there's no time.

She rises up, and the entire ceiling opens into a wonderful light. She springs off her altar, bounding up into the light, and disappears.

Edward and I stand there, dumbstruck, staring up at the ceiling. When we look back down, we see the golden statue back on the altar. But now it's still and lifeless.

Finally, I snap out of my daze, remembering our task. We have to get this Ruby Tablet to Heinrich fast, before he does something terrible to Lux. Edward and I wheel the silver cart out of the room. Just before we reach the final set of golden doors, I pause and look down at the Alliance ring. Quickly, I remove it and shove it into the depths of my backpack.

When we push through the doors, there in the hallway are Heinrich, Greta, and Pickle the white crocodile. We don't see Lux anywhere.

"Well, well!" Heinrich says in a greasy voice. "We thought you were dead!"

"Where's Lux?" I ask him, looking around for her.

"Where's my Ruby Tablet?" he says, ignoring my question.

We wheel the silver cart forward. Heinrich unwraps the muslin, carefully studying the tablet.

"Yes," he whispers. He gives us a mean grin. "You have

done well, my little lumps of clay. Now I shall reward you for your efforts."

Greta and Pickle lead us up the marble ramp and across the sea-green lake on the raised walkway. We see Lux tied to a pillar by the necropolis. She has a gag in her mouth. When she sees us, she struggles to get loose.

As soon as we reach her, Heinrich removes the gag.

"Jerk!" she spits at him angrily.

Pickle hisses.

"This one talks a lot," Heinrich says with a sigh, untying Lux's ropes.

As soon as she's free, Lux rushes to Edward and me. We all embrace. Then Lux wheels around and faces Heinrich again.

"I talk a lot? *You* talk a lot!" she shouts. "You sausage-brained monster!"

Ignoring Lux, he turns to me and claps his hands, rubbing them together. "So!" he says. "First things first, my little wormy cheese rind: zee ring."

"The ring?" I look over at Edward. "Um, I had to leave it behind."

"What?" Heinrich looks shocked.

Edward looks a little shocked too, but he tries to cover it up.

"I had to give it to the sphinx," I say.

Heinrich sits down on a rock and eyes me suspiciously. "Lies," he says calmly. "You are telling me lies!"

I shake my head. "You don't think I could solve a sphinx's riddle, do you? I had to give her the ring so we could get the Ruby Tablet past her!"

He narrows his eyes. "Well . . ."

"He's a stupid little wormy cheese rind, remember?" Edward adds, catching on to the act.

Heinrich reluctantly buys it. "If you are lying," he says

menacingly, "I will find out."

"Sounds super," I say. "So, can we go now?"

"No. I'm sorry, my little rotten tater tots, but I'm afraid you cannot."

Pickle hisses at us as Heinrich takes out his gun and points it at us. We start backing up toward the necropolis, until we stumble into a large dark tomb.

"You should be excited, my little tarantulas," Heinrich says. "You're so lucky! You get to experience a cursed tomb firsthand!"

"There's no such thing as a cursed tomb," Edward says.

"Yes. OK!" Heinrich spits. "Just like there's no *magic stereopticon!*"

He lets out a big belly laugh, then barks German commands at Pickle. The croc chomps down on a thick rope attached to a massive chunk of granite. He drags the granite in front of the tomb's door.

"Don't worry, children!" Heinrich shouts as the door closes. "You will not be lonely for long! Say hello to zee shabtis for me!"

Bit by bit, the door is closing.

"We'll escape, you know!" Edward shouts back at him. "There are hundreds of ways out of every tomb, and I know all of them! You Germans don't know the first thing about engineering! We'll be out by dawn! You'd better—"

BA-BOOM!

The tomb's granite seal locks in place.

I light a flare from my backpack, and we look around the gloomy space. There's a lone sarcophagus in the center of the tomb. The big white granite coffin is flanked by two statues of Anubis holding long iron spears. The walls are covered with faded hieroglyphs. Other than that, there's nothing.

CHAPTER TEN

"Was any of that true?" I ask Edward. "Are there hundreds of ways out of every tomb?"

"No," Edward says. "Absolutely not. We're going to die in here."

"Stop it, Edward." Lux turns to me. "I don't understand. How could you guys give Heinrich the Ruby Tablet? Don't you know what he can do with it? He can destroy the whole world!"

"We didn't give it to him," I say with a small smile. "We gave him a duplicate."

"A duplicate?"

"The less you know, the better, Lux."

"But what happens when Heinrich finds out?" she presses. "He'll kill us."

"Actually," Edward says with a sigh, looking around the tomb, "I believe he already has."

"Come on, guys," Lux says. "We're not going to die. Not yet. AZ, got another flare?"

I shake my head. "Nope. This is my last one. But wait—I have sparklers!"

I dig into my backpack, then hand them each a sparkler. Thank goodness I saved a few packs from Fourth of July. We light them and gather around the ever-shrinking circle of light.

"I'm starving," Lux says. "I don't mind dying, but I don't want to die hungry."

"No need to be hungry!" I tell her. "There's always something to eat."

I rummage around the gritty stones at the tomb's base until I find my prize, a wriggling insect. I hold it up between my fingers.

Edward frowns at me. "Is that a *Scolopendra cingulata*?"

I shrug. "Dunno. Is that a stupid science name for an Egyptian centipede?"

"Exactly."

"Well, I call it a wriggly protein bar!" I hold the centipede up over my mouth and bite it in half. "Delicious! Crunchy too. You guys want one?"

I catch another centipede, even bigger than the first.

"Come on—just try one. Didn't all those old explorers eat weird stuff on expeditions? Livingstone and those guys? You think they were having scones in the jungle? Come on!"

Lux folds her arms in front of her. "Nope. No way. I guess I would rather starve."

"Edward, how about you?" I ask. "Actually, you already ate some centipedes today. Remember those crunchy pancakes?"

He shoots me a look of disgust and shock, then he shrugs. "I *am* hungry," he admits. "All right. I'll do it," he says, wrinkling his nose. "But only in the name of science."

Lux looks alarmed. "Edward, don't!"

"Come on," I coach him. "Just hold it like this, and drop it in."

"Stop rushing me!"

Edward pauses, then bites into the centipede. His eyes open wide. He starts spitting and turns a frightful shade of green. Then he vomits all over the floor.

After that, I don't offer anyone any more centipedes.

We spring into action, trying to find a way out. We push on every stone, every inch, hoping to trigger a hidden doorway or secret panel. We sparingly use sparklers, taking turns keeping one lit at all times. We're mostly in the dark now, but our eyes have plenty of time to adjust. The minutes drag on. Maybe even hours. It's hard to tell.

It gets warm in the tomb. Really warm. Like we are baking inside an oven set on low. We get dehydrated and fuzzy. The air seems to get thicker—there isn't enough oxygen. Sweat beads up on my forehead. There has to be a way out!

I drop to my knees and crawl along the floor. With one hand, I hold a sparkler, as it's my turn to provide light. With my other hand, I slide my fingers across the seams between the sandy stones, looking desperately for a hidden latch or secret trigger. There has to be a hidden door somewhere, a secret escape tunnel, right? There always is in the movies.

But this isn't the movies. This is horribly real.

Just then, the tomb goes pitch-black. I've been so focused on searching the floor that I didn't even notice my sparkler dying out.

"Hey!" Edward and Lux both call out at the same time.

"Someone light up a new sparkler," Lux says with a sigh.

I can hear Edward fumble with his. "Hold on—I can't find it!"

We're plunged into complete darkness for the first time. I don't know why, but all I feel is fear—raw, howling fear. The kind that comes when you're in a very, very bad situation.

Then we hear something.

Rishhhhhitttta!

"What's that sound?" Lux asks. "Did you hear it?"

Rishhhhhitttta!

"There it is again!"

As Edward's sparkler ignites, I squint into the dim light. "I don't see anything."

"Me either," Edward says nervously.

"Something just ran past me!" Lux shouts.

"What was it?" I ask. "A cockroach?"

"*Bigger!*"

"A mouse?" Edward asks.

"Um . . . are Egyptian mice *blue*?"

"Blue?"

Rishhhhhitttta!

"There it is again!" she shouts.

I jump back as I see a small blue thing scurry across our ring of light. "I saw one!" I shout.

In the dim circle of light from the sparkler, we can't see much. But we can make out vague little shapes in the shadows. Sometimes we see a flash of blue.

Lux backs up slowly. "Um, Edward? What was that word Heinrich used before he shut the door? He said, 'Say hello to the *shabby*-somethings'?"

"Oh . . . shabtis?" asks Edward.

I recognize the word now. "Those are funeral statues, right? We saw them in the museum."

He nods. "Correct."

Rishhhhhitttttta! Rishhhhhitttttta!

"Are they supposed to . . . move?" Lux asks, staring into the shadows.

"Well, legend says shabtis can come to life in the dark."

I swallow hard.

The sparkler flickers against the wall, and we hear *Rishhhhhitttttta! Rishhhhhitttttta!* More turquoise flashes streak past.

"What was that?" Edward shouts.

"Stand near the light!" Lux shouts. "We're safe as long as there's light."

That's when my sparkler fizzles out, casting the room into inky darkness.

"Of course," Lux says with a sigh.

On the floor nearby, we hear a pitter-patter, like ominous raindrops.

Rishhhhhitttttta! Rishhhhhitttttta! Rishhhhhitttttta!

"I felt something on my leg!" Edward yells.

We clutch at each other and jump up onto the sarcophagus in the center of the tomb. The pitter-patter gets louder as

hundreds of little feet start rushing into the room.

"Just stay calm!" Lux says. "We'll be okay up here!"

Suddenly, Edward screams as something climbs up onto the sarcophagus.

Lux gives it a swift kick. "Never mind! We need to get out of here!" she shouts.

"We need *them* to get out of here!" Edward shrieks.

Blindly, I scrounge inside my backpack, searching for another sparkler. I feel only two left. More importantly, I feel something else that might help us. I light a sparkler, then hurry to dig out a small yellow bottle and a large green bottle.

"What's that?" Lux shouts.

"Just hold this," I tell her, handing her the green bottle. "And aim it into the room! Hold it tight! This is gonna get messy!"

"What on earth are you doing now?" Edward shouts. "They're coming!"

As Lux holds the large green bottle, I quickly pour the contents of the small yellow bottle into it.

BOOM!

A volcano of glowing green foam blasts from the bottle Lux is holding. I have to keep her from stumbling backward.

"Aim at them!" I shout. "Aim it at the shabtis!"

Brilliantly, she hoses down the sea of little blue men below us with gallons and gallons of Master Blaster Exploding Foam.

It's awesome.

But what happens next is not awesome. As the foam begins to fizzle away, the swamped shabtis begin to stir.

"We have to hide," Lux says.

"Where?" I look around the empty tomb.

"In the sarcophagus," she says. "Come with me!"

CHAPTER TEN

She jumps down, and we follow her. She grabs an iron spear from one of the statues of Anubis standing nearby. She then jams the spear in the top seam of the huge granite box.

"What are you doing?" Edward asks nervously.

"Opening this thing. C'mon, AZ—grab the other spear and give me a hand."

I hurry to get the other spear. Together, we pry up the heavy granite lid.

"Stop!" Edward protests. "That's a priceless artifact you're desecrating!"

"Oh yeah?" Lux snorts. "Well, either *we* desecrate it, or those things desecrate *us*!"

Edward glances across the room at the hundreds of shabtis slowly rising and emerging from the settling foam. His eyes go wide. Then he turns around and quickly helps me with the spear I'm holding, pressing his full weight on it too.

The lid moves.

"Not too far now, guys!" Lux shouts. "We just want to open it enough so we can get in!"

"The shabtis are coming," Edward shouts. "Hurry!"

We manage to shove the granite lid off enough so we can climb inside. Then we hunch over and use our backs to lift and move the lid back in place.

"Not all the way!" Lux whispers. "We need to breathe!"

We drop the lid with a loud clunk just as the first wave of shabtis hit. They angrily reach their little blue arms in through the crack we left open so we can breathe.

"Why don't they leave us alone?" Lux says.

She reaches down for her Tecpatl knife, then swipes at the menacing little blue arms. The shabtis howl and squeal as they run off into the shadowy tomb.

Just as my sparkler starts to fizzle out, I dig in my backpack for a new one. The last one.

"Um . . . we're still not alone," Edward says, looking down.

Beneath us on the floor of the sarcophagus is a mummy. But it's smaller than mummies you usually see. It's only three feet long. Tucked next to the mummy is a doll and some small trinkets.

While Lux and I scramble away from it, Edward takes my sparkler and studies the mummy's petite frame with great interest.

"Who was the mummy?" Lux asks. "Can you tell?"

"I think it's a young girl. Probably a royal princess." He looks closer. "Oh, there's a smaller mummy here too. I wonder if it might be a younger sibling."

He gingerly investigates, pulling back the wrapping on the smaller mummy. We all scream when the hideous face of her pet baboon leers out at us.

"Maybe that's why the tomb is cursed," I whisper.

Suddenly, the sparkler reaches its end. We all look up to see the light sputter out.

We sit in complete darkness. All night.

It's the longest night of my life. Fear pools in my stomach. As the long hours drag on, it dawns on me that whatever time we have left may not be enough. The question isn't whether there's a way out of this tomb. It's whether we can even find it in time, before we starve to death or die from dehydration.

Grim reality floods my brain like cold black water. A terrible thought grows in my head, like a freight train barreling down a long dark tunnel. We might *die* in here, and no one would ever know what happened to us. All the amazing things we've seen, all the unbelievable events we've witnessed—they would all be lost forever. One day, maybe thousands of years from now, some future archaeologists might find our bones and tag them with dates and numbers, but nothing more.

Then the freight train in my head bursts from the tunnel. The body in this sarcophagus isn't just an "artifact" or even a "mummy."

She was a real person. A young girl. An actual person, just like us.

We have to find a way out of here. I can't believe I ever wanted to go on an adventure. Some adventure this has been. I'm not the world's greatest explorer I thought I was. We haven't been lucky or smart or ingenious. We've been tricked, threatened at gunpoint, and entombed here without the benefit of first being dead.

We've been buried alive.

CHAPTER ELEVEN
THE DEAD AWAKEN

I wake up. It's pitch black. We're still here in the sarcophagus, still trapped in a tomb. Aching, I manage to sit up.

Lux groans beside me, waking up too. "What happened?" she asks groggily. "Was that a dream?"

"More like a nightmare," I tell her. "Only it's real."

Edward coughs. In the darkness, he asks me, "Any breakfast, before we die?"

I dig around in my pockets and put together a meager breakfast of coconut canteens and dried mulberries, three for each of us. We eat silently in the dark.

Then I hear something. "What was that?" I whisper.

"What?" Lux looks around.

The sound comes again. "*That!* Are those voices? *Sh!* Listen!"

CHAPTER ELEVEN

They *are* voices, outside the tomb, getting louder and more distinct. They're speaking some foreign language. A wild tangle of fear and hope gets caught like a lump in my throat. I can hardly breathe.

Then we hear strange clanking sounds that get louder and louder. A heavy stone is being dragged across the floor. I think it's the granite that was blocking the tomb entrance. Now a sliver of light shines in from the crack in the sarcophagus lid. Shadows pass along the wall.

We scramble to lift the sarcophagus lid up an inch so we can peer out. We see a man walk in. He has dark skin and dark eyes, and he wears a short white kilt. He's carrying metal pails filled with colorful powders. He sets them down by the wall. He might be a painter.

"Who's that?" I whisper.

Edward doesn't know. "Think he works for Heinrich?" he wonders.

"Look!" Lux says. "Here comes another one!"

A second man comes in carrying a roll of canvas. He spreads it out next to the painter.

"What's going on?" Edward whispers. "Who are they?"

All of a sudden, I figure it out. "They're workers! Ancient Ophirian workers!" I turn excitedly to Edward. "Remember what the sphinx said?"

"You're right!" Edward says, his eyes wide.

"Wait—what did the sphinx say about what?" Lux quickly asks. "You have to get me up to speed. I was all tied up, remember?"

"The sphinx said the city would come to life for one more day to honor her death!"

We watch in awe as more workers pour in. Painters, builders, and stonecutters going back to work, just as they had centuries ago.

"This means all the doors are open!" I tell them. "All we have to do is get up to the surface!"

Suddenly, an angry voice starts shouting. When we peer through the crack in the lid, we see white linen fabric coming right at us. Next thing we know, the granite lid—which is much whiter and newer looking now—slides off.

The three of us look up at an official-looking Ophirian man wearing a long white tunic. He's shouting at us loudly.

"Edward, what's he saying?" I ask.

Edward squints up at the man. "Um . . . I don't exactly know what he's saying, but I get the sense he's an overseer or something. I don't think we should be in here."

The man shouts at us again. Even I know he's telling us to get out of the sarcophagus.

I scramble out, grabbing my yellow backpack. That's when I notice all traces of the mummy girl are gone. The baboon is gone too. The sarcophagus is empty. I don't have time to wonder about it, though. The man in the white tunic points angrily at the door and shoos us out of the tomb.

Other workers escort us up to the river, where a large boat is being loaded. We're ushered on board, and the boat takes us up a winding canal back to the pink lake. We get off the boat and join another crowd of people.

I can't believe it. Here I was, wanting to be a great explorer, to rescue artifacts and treasure from the past, and now the past is rescuing me. Ancient Ophirians have saved me from being buried alive.

We travel through the city, which is now teeming with Ophirians going about their ancient daily lives. In the industrial district, workers at the wabet are cutting linen for funeral wraps. Brewers are fermenting barley for beer. Brick workers are mixing clay with straw. Perfumers are wringing cloth sacks of flower petals. We see glassblowers and goldsmiths and potters.

The kiln at the pottery studio is smoking, and all the wheels are spinning as potters throw enormous terra-cotta vases. A worker inspects them. He smashes a vase to pieces when it isn't perfect.

"I want that job!" Lux says. "You get to smash stuff all day!"

We see stone carvers chiseling ivory statues, cobblers stitching papyrus sandals, jewelers polishing pendants, and pharmacists dispensing medicine from large white alabaster jars. In the cosmetics shop, ladies try on kohl eyeliner and scented wigs. One of them is buying the same wig I tried on.

Ophirians fill the streets. Children play in fountains, and servants hurry about their chores. We see priests anointing statues and scribes copying religious texts. We see students outside the house of life practicing their hieroglyphs on plaster tablets.

In the open-air market, the clay-brick ovens now smoke happily, preparing an unending array of delicious-smelling food. We see sacks of grain, blocks of salt, barrels of beer, bottles of olive oil, pots of honey, and baskets of fish. There are also racks of lamb meat, roasted duck, stuffed figs, and sweet honey

cakes. I suddenly remember that I am very hungry.

Everywhere we look, vendors crouch on woven reed mats, selling their wares. We see oil lamps, papyrus rolls, cypress chairs, bronze cookware, and terra-cotta dishware. We're surrounded by smoking incense, rare cassia perfume, frankincense and myrrh, pots of eye paint, blocks of black kohl, and polished mirrors. There are carved amulets, golden bracelets, beaded necklaces, turquoise scarabs, glass bottles, bronze ingots, polished agates, red carnelians, lapis lazulis. There are ostrich feathers, ibis eggs, leopard skins, lion skins, ivory elephant tusks, pet baboons, domesticated horses, and hand-carved chariots.

We're transfixed by this ancient city come to life. For a long time, we just wander around, trying to take it all in. But while we're enjoying the past, Lux reminds us about our present danger.

"Come on," she says. "We really should get out of the city! Heinrich could come back any minute!"

Edward nods. "Right. Let's get above ground, then we can figure out what to do next."

We hurry back up the Royal Road. But when we reach the entrance at the statue of Taharqa, another overseer stops us. He assumes we belong to a nearby group of foreigners. He angrily steers us back into the group.

Once again, we find ourselves unable to leave. It's not all

bad news, though. After careful observation and study, Edward discovers we have joined a group of well-respected merchants from Syria.

"They've been invited to the pharaoh's grand feast in honor of the sphinx," he explains.

"Feast?" I perk up.

"We should lie low and stick with these merchants," Lux says. "Then we can make a break for it after the feast."

I nod. I don't care what the plan is. I'm just happy we're eating.

Before the feast, we are treated to incredible entertainment. We watch archery competitions and chariot races. There's also a spectacular regatta on the luminous pink lake. Ships made of silver and sporting blue linen sails try to sink each other in a mock battle. The citizens of Ophir cheer and applaud during the finale, and a sudden explosion of fireworks concludes the show.

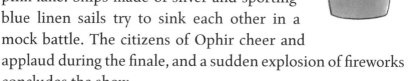

"I like how these people throw a funeral!" I shout over the racket.

Afterward, our group is led to the palace—where we camped just the night before. Now the hall is filled with Ophirians and distinguished guests gathering for the grand feast. Burning incense makes the air smoky as servant girls drape the guests with wreaths of fragrant flowers and pour perfumed water on their hands.

We're ushered into the long banquet hall and seated on woven-reed mats at low tables. Tall jugs of water and basins stand nearby, in case we want to wash our hands again.

Monkeys with jewel-studded collars shriek and race

around the tables. Acrobats, musicians, and dancers perform on the recessed stages set between the banquet hall columns.

Then a horn sounds.

The crowd hushes, and everyone turns to the balcony overlooking the banquet hall. There above us appears a magnificent figure.

"It's Pharaoh Taharqa," Edward whispers in awe.

Taharqa wears exotic animal furs, fine linen trimmed in gold, and an enormous blue headdress with a gold cobra coiled around it. Heavy black paint frames his eyes, and his muscular arms are covered with tattoos.

While the pharaoh greets his people, the priests anoint a large golden statue of a sphinx with spices and perfumes. It's the same statue we saw in the blue chamber.

Finally, the pharaoh raises his arms, and the whole room cheers. The priests' ritual anointing is over.

I smell roasted meats and other delicious food waiting

nearby. It makes my mouth water and my stomach rumble. At last, servants circulate throughout the room with large trays of delectable dishes, many of which were at the museum. There's braised lamb, stewed figs, roasted quail, pickled catfish, pigeon casserole, fried goose livers, barbecued eel, antelope chops, wild celery, papyrus stalks, and lotus hearts. Then there's gazelle, ostrich eggs, and sweet honey . . . plus platters filled with juicy plums, ruby pomegranates, shriveled dates, and slices of pink watermelon. We sample pyramids of dried apricots and bunches of purple grapes. We count over thirty different kinds of bread.

I gnaw on a huge greasy lamb shank, holding it with both of my hands. "Now this is a portion!" I grin.

When the feast of the sphinx is over, people make their way outside to the wide boulevard in front of the palace. There, the gold statue of the sphinx is being dressed in royal robes and adorned with priceless jewels and rare perfumes. Then royal porters carry the statue on a large platform, bringing her down to the pink lake.

Under the watchful eye of our overseer, we follow the

crowd trailing after the sphinx. At the lakeshore, a golden boat awaits her. The long, narrow boat is flanked by rows of oars on each side, with men in position and at the ready.

We cheer and applaud with the crowd as the sphinx's boat is slowly launched into the water. Once again, I'm sad to see the sphinx go. But it's a fitting send-off for her.

"Well, well!" a voice suddenly says. "What do we have here?"

Heinrich!

We turn around slowly, and there he is, the super slimeball himself. He gives us a crooked smile.

"Hello, my oozing little pockmarks!"

Without warning, Lux lunges at him, giving him a good, hard shove. Heinrich topples over backward.

"Run!" she shouts at us.

We take off through the crowd. Everyone is now turning around to head back into the palace. Fighting against the crowd, we run in the opposite direction. We head along the lake and then down the long stone dock, where the sphinx's golden boat is just leaving. We run so hard I think my shinbones might split through my skin.

"Jump!" Lux shouts when we reach the end of the dock.

We leap off the dock, over the water, reaching our arms out as far as we can. We land on the deck of the sphinx's boat. We're sailing safely away from the harbor. There's no way Heinrich can catch us now.

We scramble to hide behind a stacked pyramid of colorful fruit.

"Did anyone see us jump on board?" Lux wonders.

I'm sure no one on land saw us. As for whether anyone on board saw us, I peek out at the rows of crewmen expertly rowing the boat, turning their oars with precision. They didn't see us. They're not even facing us.

The only one who could've seen us jump on the boat is the guy steering the big rudder in the back. But he's too busy shouting commands to notice three uninvited passengers.

Just then, he turns the rudder sharply. We look up, and the boat seems to be headed right for a cave wall. And to make matters worse, the rowers seem to be rowing even more quickly!

"Is he insane?" Lux whispers. "We're going to crash!"

"Should we jump?" Edward asks. "They wouldn't crash a boat they're on, would they?"

Before anyone can answer, we realize the cave wall is actually two *separate* walls staggered one over the other. Their colors match perfectly. From a distance, they create an illusion of a solid wall. But actually, they mark a hidden entrance.

The boat neatly navigates between the walls, then pulls into a small rectangular chamber. It's just big enough for our boat to float in without touching the walls.

We sigh with relief.

"Looks like we're docking," Lux says. "I bet everyone will get off the boat in a few minutes, and we can sneak off too."

Suddenly, we hear a loud KER-KLUNK! An enormous stone wall closes behind us. Then water starts pouring into the chamber.

"The water is rising." Lux looks at me, frowning. "Why is the water rising?"

"Because this isn't a *dock*," Edward tells her. "It's a *lock*."

He goes on to explain that a lock is a man-made system used to raise and lower boats between stretches of water at different levels. For instance, locks are used where the level of the water in a river changes, such as at a dam or a waterfall. It's like a watery staircase for boats.

"In this case," Edward says excitedly, "Ophirian engineers built a system of locks and dams to bring boats from the underground pink lake all the way up to the Nile!"

To prove Edward's point, our boat does in fact rise as water pours into the chamber.

CHAPTER ELEVEN

Soon, we're high enough to sail into the next chamber above us. Then more water pours in, and we're lifted up to the third chamber. Lock by lock, we travel up through miles of bedrock, all the way to the surface.

It is a marvel of ancient engineering.

"This is perfect!" Lux says. "Heinrich will be looking for us down in Ophir. But we'll be up here, on the river!"

When the sphinx's boat finally exits the last lock, we sail out into the sunset. We're floating on the Nile. There is a soft breeze. The sun sinks into the horizon, lower and lower.

"This is amazing!" I say, unable to stop smiling.

Then I hear a loud splash. We're suddenly wet and flailing in the Nile's warm water. We sputter and cough, shaking our heads and looking around. The boat, the crew, the sphinx— they've all vanished.

"They're gone!" Lux shouts at me from downstream. "The sun went down!"

"What?" I can hardly hear her.

"The city came to life for just one day. The sun went down, and now the city's gone!" she says, paddling as best she can. "And so is the boat!"

I turn around just in time to see Edward's fingertips sinking quickly underwater.

"Edward!" I shout.

I dive underwater, kicking hard against the current, my arms swinging out blindly in the murky water. I go down and down, until I think my lungs will pop. Then I hit something soft. It's either Edward or a sleeping crocodile. There's no time to guess. I grab the dark figure and kick hard for the surface.

Fortunately, it's Edward. As soon as I break through the surface, I shout, "Give me a hand! Help me get him out of here!"

"With pleasure!" a familiar voice says.

I look up.

Heinrich? Ugh—again?

There he is, standing on the deck of a massive riverboat. The boat's name is on the bow: *Port-A-Party*. Lux has already been captured and is sitting in the bow.

Heinrich smirks at me. "You'd better hand your friend over," he says, pointing to Edward in my grasp. "He's turning an ugly shade of blue."

Edward coughs and spits out a small chunk of algae. I struggle to keep him afloat, my arm hooked under his shoulder.

Then I hear a loud WHAP! A giant fishing net drops down on us. Greta scoops us up, lifting us out of the water. Heinrich claps as she lowers us into the boat.

I look over at Heinrich through the tangled net. "Just one question: You seriously named your boat *Port-A-Party*?"

CHAPTER TWELVE

THE GREAT GROSS-OFF

We're trapped inside the cabin of the boat as Heinrich speeds down the river.

"How are you doing, my little tarantulas?" he shouts down through the small hatch at us. "Don't worry—we'll be home soon!"

"Where's 'home'?" Lux whispers.

Edward and I can only shrug.

A few moments later, the boat slows down. We've arrived at a dock hidden in the reeds. Heinrich slips the *Port-A-Party* next to an airboat tied up at the dock. Then he marches us off the boat and leads us down a path through the jungle. We end up at his secret lair: a sprawling matrix of interconnected caves inside a large cliff.

Two towering marble statues greet us inside the entrance.

Beside them is a large rusty orange shipping container marked RED CROSS. The container's door is partway open, and we see Egyptian artifacts inside, including carved gold statues and ancient pots, tapestries, and jewels.

"So that's how Heinrich smuggles artifacts out of the country!" Lux whispers. "He disguises them in shipping containers marked as emergency supplies! What a slimy sneak!"

"Keep moving!" Heinrich shouts at us.

With Greta and Pickle nipping at our heels, he marches us through a labyrinth of caves, each filled with stacks of bound books, old newspapers, and stolen Egyptian artifacts: carved furniture, ancient weavings, marble statues, and ancient stone tablets. The creep has been looting archaeological sites for a while.

Heinrich brings us into a special chamber he's outfitted for the Ruby Tablet. The luminous scarlet tablet sits on a large slanted pedestal. Heinrich has clearly made his lair comfortable.

"All right, my mealworms," he says. "Tell me—why does zee Ruby Tablet not work?" His face turns as red as the tablet itself.

Edward, Lux, and I exchange looks.

"It doesn't work?" I say innocently.

"Nein!" he shouts.

"Well, you're the evil genius," I reply. "If you can't get it to work, no one can."

"I'm getting very tired of your lies," he says, his eyes hardening. "In fact, I think you have outlived your usefulness. Follow me, please."

Heinrich leads us down an ominous tunnel to an even more ominous cave with cockroaches as big as candy bars scuttling around on the floor. In the center of the cave, there's a large pit.

"Now, my shiny little piles of crocodile poo," he says with a smile, "it's time to kill you."

I look at him. "*Kill* us?"

"Of course. You're annoying, uninteresting little weasels. Well, *I* will not be killing you, exactly. It is zee crocodiles who will kill you after I throw you in."

"In *what*?" Lux asks, glaring.

"You've heard of a Crock-Pot? We have something a bit different. We have a Croc-Pit! A pit filled with hungry crocodiles. Ah, here they are now!"

He pushes us to the edge of the deep pit. We stare down the slick, gummy sides. At the bottom of the pit, we see things moving. They are hundreds of white crocodiles splashing and writhing.

Heinrich waves at them. "*Hallo*, my pretties!" he shouts

down to the crocodiles. "I brought you a tasty snack!" He turns to us. "These crocs have very discerning taste buds, just like their Uncle Heinrich. They've developed a taste for all zee unique foods I bring them."

He shoves me forward a little so the crocs can see me. I almost stumble in. The crocs thrash wildly. Lux and Edward quickly reach for me, so I don't fall into the disgusting pit. It reeks of algae and funky crocodile poo.

We can't get thrown down there!

I suddenly remember the pharaonic buffet and how particular Heinrich was about the food. I have an idea. "Um, Heinrich?" I ask.

"What?" he snaps.

"You said you had discerning tastes for unique foods?"

"Of course. I am a world traveler. I have eaten every delicacy ever known."

"AZ," Edward says in a trembling voice, "can we not talk about delicacies right now?" He glances at the crocs waiting to make us their snack.

I ignore him and look right at Heinrich. "Have you eaten whole roasted sparrows?" I ask.

He scoffs. "Love them!"

"What about grubs?"

"I sprinkle them in my cereal every morning. Excellent source of protein." He pats his belly and gives us a crooked grin. "I'm known all over zee world for my iron gut."

"So am I," I say. "I have an iron gut too."

He looks at me with a disgusted expression. "Don't be ridiculous!" he says. "You're just a small sniveling boy!"

I nervously look down into the pit. After a deep breath, I lift my chin high. "I bet my stomach is stronger than yours," I challenge.

CHAPTER TWELVE

"What?"

"I said, I bet my stomach is stronger than yours!"

"AZ!" Lux hisses. "What are you doing?"

"There is no way your feeble little worm belly is stronger than mine!" Heinrich snarls.

I lean over and pick up a dead, dried-up cockroach from the cave floor. I drop it neatly in my mouth and crunch down hard.

"This is nothing," I tell him. "I can eat way weirder food than this. I can eat anything."

"Well," he taunts, "surely not anything."

"Pretty much. I know I can eat anything you can eat."

Edward, Lux, and even Greta look at Heinrich, awaiting his response.

Heinrich does not like what he hears. "Would you eat a poisonous snake?" he asks quickly.

The others look back at me. It's as if they were watching a tennis match.

"Sure," I say. "Already eaten plenty."

"Would you eat a jellied rat?"

"No problem."

He squints hard at me. "So, you think your gut is more ironclad than mine?"

I shrug. "Only one way to find out."

"How?" He arches an eyebrow.

"We have a gross-off."

"A *what*-off?"

"A gross-off. It's like a game."

A tiny glint shines in Heinrich's eye, and the corner of his mouth turns up ever so slightly. "What kind of game?"

"Yes, AZ—what kind of game?" Lux is giving me the look.

"It's a cooking contest. A battle of wits, skill, and the

ability to eat gross things. It's a quick-fire cook-off with bonus points for being gross."

"How do we do this gross-off?" Heinrich asks, his interest suddenly growing.

"It's easy. We each cook three dishes, using any ingredients we want. The grosser, the better. Then we serve our dishes to each other and see who can finish the entire meal—and who can't. Whoever has three clean plates wins." I pause for dramatic effect. "And whoever pukes loses."

Heinrich scratches his chin as he considers this. Everyone is quiet and still. I'm not sure Edward and Lux are even breathing.

"So, I make you a meal?" Heinrich repeats. "And you make me a meal?"

"Yep. Three courses of the grossest food imaginable—an appetizer, a main dish, and a dessert. We'll cook at the same time, in the same kitchen, just like those celebrity chefs on TV."

"Please," he scoffs. "I'm a better chef than any of those orangutans wearing aprons!"

"Well, of course you're better," I say. "But I'm good too. I may even be better than you."

"Ha!" he says indignantly.

I shrug, casually examining my dirty fingernails. "Well, we both know there's only one way to find out who's better at preparing and eating gross food. Of course," I add with a sweet smile, "if you're insecure about it, I completely understand."

"*Insecure?*" he growls. "I'll show you who's insecure, my little termite. So be it! Let zee great gross-off begin. Prepare to eat zee grossest food ever made!" Fully committed now, Heinrich announces the rules: "We will have one hour to assemble all our ingredients. They must be gathered from zee jungle or from my pantry, where I have stockpiled zee most obscure ingredients from all over zee world. Then we'll have only one hour to cook zee meal. Agreed?"

I nod. "Agreed."

Heinrich takes out a silver whistle and blows it so loudly we all clamp our hands over our ears. Seconds later, the doors burst open, and a swarm of little monkeys rushes in. They wear red velvet vests and matching red velvet gumdrop-shaped hats that accentuate their mean little red eyes. They carry trays of food and water.

"These are my monkey butlers," Heinrich says proudly.

"Your . . . *what?*" Lux stares at them.

A monkey butler spins around and shrieks at us, exposing a horrific row of sharp teeth. If they weren't so nasty, I would've felt sorry for them, having to do Heinrich's bidding and wear those ridiculous uniforms. They hiss at us as they dart around. They also shriek anytime they make a mistake, which is constantly. They nip and slap at each other, causing trays to topple over. A pitcher of water crashes to the floor. Whatever food they drop, they then throw at each other.

They're terrible butlers.

Heinrich blows his whistle again and assigns five especially hyperactive monkeys to "help" me—which apparently means to drop things, shriek, and race around.

"They will escort you into zee jungle and assure your return," he tells me.

"Don't worry," I say. "I'll come back."

"Oh, I know you will," he sneers. "Because I'll have your

little friends here locked up nice and tight in captivity! I don't think we need these two for our contest. We can find better things for them to do."

Edward, Lux, and I share worried glances.

Just then, two monkeys collide into each other. Trays, pitchers, and food go flying. A particularly heavy platter lands right on Greta's foot. She doubles over, reaching for her toes and hopping in pain. "That's it, I'm going to my room!" she shouts.

Heinrich begins barking at the monkeys in German, which makes the monkeys screech. He gets louder and louder, and so do they. Meanwhile, Greta limps off, wincing in pain and muttering about the monkeys. Pickle follows her like a worried puppy.

It's the perfect distraction.

"Don't worry," I quickly tell Edward and Lux. "I have a plan."

"Well, you'd better have a plan!" Edward hisses. "Why are you monkeying around with cooking contests?" He clears his throat. "No pun intended."

"AZ, we have to get out of here!" Lux implores.

"That's exactly what I'm trying to do!"

Heinrich blows his whistle, and the monkey butlers at last quiet down. He gives some orders, and the five monkey butlers assigned to me scurry off. When they return, they have outfitted themselves with scary-looking tranquilizer guns.

"Don't worry. They won't shoot you—unless you try to escape!" He pauses and frowns. "But be careful. They don't always seem to know when someone is trying to escape and when they're just walking in a different direction. There have been incidents . . ." He waves his hands. "Forget it. I'm sure everything will be fine."

CHAPTER TWELVE

With that, he claps his hands.

"Let zee gross-off begin!"

Heinrich hurries off, heading through the maze of caves. I start after him, only to stop in my tracks when I see monkey butlers swarm Edward and Lux and force them into another room.

"Go, AZ! Go!" Lux shouts as they disappear.

Adrenaline surges as I take off like a flash. I catch up with Heinrich as we make our way out of the caves. My escorts shriek at my heels. I expect a tranquilizer in the back at any time.

Heinrich goes one way and I the other once we hit the jungle. I run recklessly through the thick vegetation. I know this gross-off was my grand plan, but now I have no idea what to get or what to look for. My brain's a jumbled sloppy mess.

I'm ankle-deep in river mud and covered with bug bites when I see a brilliant flash of green. I get a potentially great—or possibly horrible—idea. I take out an empty bug jar and creep stealthily through the jungle with it poised for the catch. I can only hope the monkeys don't interpret it as an attempt to escape.

By the time I return to Heinrich's kitchen, my feet are aching from running and climbing trees and scaling rocks. Not only do I ache but my brain is starting to blister too. My secret plan requires something I hate, something that should be banned from all kitchens.

Math.

That's right—my recipe requires math. Exact portions and measurements. I need to work it all out precisely before I even begin cooking. If I make even one wrong calculation, the whole plan will be a disaster, and we'll end up as Pickle kibble.

I slowly and painfully calculate my recipe in my adventure

journal. But I keep running into dead ends. I scribble, then scratch out numbers. I rip pages out of my journal and crumple them up.

If only I had memorized a few things—my multiplication tables or percentages—I could blow through this. Edward would blow through this! He could solve this stupid math problem with one hand and draw an exact replica of the Great Pyramid of Giza with the other, all the while reciting *The Iliad*.

With a loud moan, I rip out another sheet of paper and crumple it up.

Heinrich exits the pantry with an armful of mysterious ingredients. He sees me and smirks. "Not going so well, my little fungus?"

"It's going just fine," I growl.

"So much scribbling," he says, nodding to my journal, "and so little cooking. Be careful—you have only a half hour left before zee great gross-off feast is served!"

Chuckling, he goes back to the stove to gleefully stir a bubbling pot of something that smells like rotting eels. He wipes his hands on his apron covered with little embroidered strawberries.

"Will you excuse me?" he asks with a sugary smile. "I must go check on zee quite wonderful, and very awful, ingredient still hissing in zee pantry."

Once he leaves, I turn back to my recipe calculations. At last, I think I have the measurements figured out. I think . . . I make myself compute everything twice and then a third time, for good measure. It all holds up.

It's time to cook.

I finish my meal moments before I hear Heinrich's whistle. The hour is up. Dinner is served.

Heinrich leads me down a maze of dark hallways to

another ominous-looking cave. There, a long crystal table is elegantly set with polished silver and porcelain plates. The room is lit by hundreds of glowing silver lanterns hanging from the ceiling. The lanterns flicker slightly in the darkness, throwing a mosaic of intricate patterns across the walls and table.

Lux and Edward are already at the table, tied with rope to their chairs. Greta is nowhere to be seen—likely still sulking in her room.

"And now, my little rotten sausages," Heinrich says, "it's dinnertime! If you don't mind, I thought we'd start with a palate cleanser before we get to zee three courses."

I shrug. "Fine."

"Oh, do we get to eat too?" Lux asks excitedly. "I'm starving."

When a monkey butler sets a plate of Heinrich's first course in front of me, she changes her mind.

"What *is* that?" she whispers. She stares at the small lump of shiny, translucent gray matter in the middle of my plate.

"This is jellied elephant mucus," Heinrich says. "It's easiest to eat with a spoon."

He orders a plate for himself, then sucks the glob of gray matter down whole. He lets out a satisfying belch.

"Yes, a wonderful palate cleanser," he says.

Edward looks doubtfully at the gray glop. "Looks like it could use a *cleanse* itself," he whispers.

I just shrug and slurp my jellied elephant mucus down. It tastes like salty jellyfish.

Lux gapes at me. "You just ate *snot*," she says.

"Yep. Wasn't bad either."

"High in protein and low in calories," Heinrich says. "And now, let's bring out zee first course for my little hungry friend."

A monkey butler sets down my first course—the appetizer.

It's served on a silver plate with a domed silver lid.

"Now, this I know you will like!" Heinrich says. "I've never met anyone who didn't eat every bite!"

The monkey butler lifts the silver lid. There on my plate is a steamy bowl of a special soup.

Edward screams and almost falls off his chair.

Lux closes her eyes. "I'm gonna be sick," she croaks.

I just smile at my bowl. "Is that scorpion soup?"

"Scorpion *and eyeball* soup," Heinrich corrects.

Just then, a big bloodshot cow eyeball floats to the surface of my soup.

"Wow," I say with a nod. "This is a freak show in a bowl."

Heinrich smiles at me. "You don't have to eat it, my little ringworm."

"No, no—I'll eat it. At least, I'll try to."

I start shoveling the soft-boiled scorpions into my mouth, careful not to eat the very tip of their tails, which are sometimes still venomous. Other than that, the scorpions are delicious. They have a woody, nutty flavor, and they're perfectly simmered in their creamy white broth.

"Thirsty?" Heinrich asks me.

A monkey appears with a white ceramic pitcher and pours a bright-red liquid into my goblet.

"It's blood," Heinrich says. "Zee Maasai drink blood from their cattle on special occasions."

I stare at my frothy red glass. "Um, OK."

I know I have an iron gut, but suddenly I gulp nervously. Maybe I'm in over my head here. My hand trembles ever so slightly as I take a tiny sip of the warm, thick liquid in my cup. I sip, then force a smile.

"Pretty good!" I say, but then I start coughing. Thankfully, everything stays down.

Next is the main course. It's a pupu platter of disgusting bites, some of which I don't even recognize. Whatever confidence I had coming into this gross-off is quickly vanishing.

"That one there is a live rhino beetle larva," Heinrich says.

He points to the huge white worm wriggling on my plate. It's as thick as my thumb and has large black eyes that seem to watch me.

"Let's see—what else?" Heinrich says, continuing. "Oh, we have monkey-dung pellets, courtesy of my friends over here," he says, gesturing to the monkey butlers. "And roasted wasps, a grasshopper taco, a grub kabob . . ."

He goes on and on, but I stop listening. I'm staring at the center of the awful plate—there's a big black hairy spider. It's been roasted and lightly sprinkled with oil.

"Is that a tarantula?" I ask. My voice cracks a bit.

"Indeed," Heinrich says. "We used to deep-fry our tarantulas, as they do in Cambodia, but now we oven-roast them. I'm watching my cholesterol," he adds.

The table is silent. Everyone watches as I pierce the hideous black spider with my fork. Black juice spurts out.

I close my eyes. I open my mouth wide, lift my fork, and shove the spider in. I chomp down so hard that bitter, inky juice runs down both sides of my face.

Edward leans over and throws up on the floor.

With the tarantula down the hatch, my confidence returns. I can do this. It takes me over an hour to eat everything on the plate—but I finish.

Finally, the monkey butlers serve dessert: an ice-cream sundae. Only this sundae has ice-cream flavors like chocolate caterpillar, vanilla grub, and strawberry 'n' creamed slugs. The creamed slugs are not delicious. But once again, I finish everything. My iron gut isn't letting me down.

I am the *grossest* explorer in the world.

Heinrich narrows his eyes at me. Clearly, he's not happy to see clean plates. If I'm not mistaken, he looks a little nervous. And he should be.

Now, it's my turn to serve Heinrich.

"I made only one course," I tell him. "I put every drop of my training, talent, and culinary know-how into this one dish."

I watch as two monkey butlers enter with covered silver plates. One sets a plate on the sideboard next to the table. The other sets a plate in front of Heinrich and removes the silver lid.

Heinrich leans forward. Edward and Lux lean forward. Even the other monkey butlers lean forward.

They're all staring at the plate.

"Is that a gumdrop?" Heinrich asks, peering down at the small green candy sitting in the center of my plate.

"Yes." I nod. "It's a gumdrop."

"What *kind* of gumdrop?" he asks slowly.

"That's a surprise," I say.

He stares at the gumdrop for a moment, then bursts out laughing. He snaps up the gumdrop with one of his spotty claws.

"One gumdrop? I prepare a feast of zee most vile foods known to man—and you make one little gumdrop? You are so stupid!"

I'm silent as he tosses the green gumdrop into his mouth.

"You think this is a challenge? Your brain is made of crabmeat! I can't wait to . . . to . . ." His eyes fill with panic. "What is this? My tongue is . . . *swellinth upth!*' he slurred.

He gasps. Sure enough, his tongue is expanding and growing like a marshmallow in the microwave.

"What's happening to him?" Lux exclaims. "AZ, what kind of gumdrop was that? Jalapeño?"

"No." I shake my head. "It's actually a *poison dart frog gumdrop.*"

I lift the silver dome off the plate on the sideboard. Out

hops the brilliant green tree frog that supplied the secret ingredient.

With that, Heinrich keels over and passes out cold, his big fat face flat on his plate.

The monkey butlers all shriek and scream. At first, I think they're going to kill us. But instead, they start screaming with joy, hugging each other and grabbing food from the sideboards.

While they celebrate, I hurry to untie Edward and Lux.

"Did you *kill* him?" Edward whispers.

"No." I pause. "Well, at least I don't *think* so. I nearly drove myself crazy figuring out the precise measurement that would knock him unconscious but not kill him."

I suppose I'd better check. I feel a pulse and see his chest rise and fall with breaths.

"No. Not dead. Just asleep."

"How long until he wakes up?" Lux asks.

"No idea. Come on—let's get out of here before we find out!"

I lunge for my backpack, and we take off running, dashing through the piles of artifacts and old books. A newspaper on top of a nearby pile catches my eye. An idea strikes. I grab the paper, roll it up, and shove it in my back pocket before taking off again.

We make our way through the front entrance of the building and sprint through the jungle.

"This way!" Edward shouts. "This way to the river!"

At the river, we scramble into the airboat tied up to the old rickety dock. Lux starts the engine, ripping the boat away from the dock without even untying the ropes. She guns it, pushing it to top speed. We race up the river as fast as we can, but within moments, we hear a deafening, thundering rumble on the water.

The *Port-A-Party* is upon us.

"No way! How could he have woken up so quickly?" Edward shouts over the noise of the boats. "Do you think it's Greta driving?"

"No time to figure it out," Lux answers, her face hard as a stone.

A fairly experienced captain, Lux uses every evasive maneuver she can think of. Lux veers toward the rocks and cuts back on the throttle, hoping the *Port-A-Party* can't turn as quickly. She zigzags across the water, creating chaotic, tumultuous waves, hoping to swamp it. She ramps the throttle and jumps shallow riverbeds, hoping it'll get stuck. She even spins the boat like a top and then jets forward, spraying the other boat with water.

But the *Port-A-Party* matches our airboat maneuver for maneuver. In fact, it gains on us. We can't outrace it. We need another plan.

I turn to Edward. "Will the stereopticon work with any photo?"

"What?" he shouts.

"The stereopticon—will it work with any photo?" I shout back.

"I'm not sure," he says, shaking his head. "Why?"

"Wait—what's that sound?" Lux interrupts.

We hear it too. It's a rumbling thunder that gets louder and louder. Lux veers the boat starboard, nearly running into the rocks. The thunder is from a waterfall, a precipice where the entire river pours over a ridge of jutting rocks. The water cascades down into a monstrous cauldron at least two hundred feet below. We flounder at the edge, with Lux doing everything she can to keep us back.

"Edward, look at this!"

I pull out the newspaper I snatched from Heinrich's cave. It's soggy and torn, but I shove it in front of him. It's not from

1930. It's from the day I arrived in London with Uncle Arthur. On the front page is an article announcing Heinrich's exhibit that night.

And there's a photo of the Egyptian Hall in the British Museum.

Edward looks at me hopefully.

"Guys, what do we do?" Lux shouts.

We look up as the shadow of the *Port-A-Party* falls over us. Without a word, Edward carefully rips out the photo of the museum while I dig in my backpack. I pull out the stereopticon, and he jams the photo in.

"Grab my hand!" I shout. "Quick! Grab my hand!"

"But the boat will go over!" Lux says desperately, still cranking on the steering wheel as we hover dangerously close to the edge of the waterfall.

"Let it!" I shout.

I hold out my hand, and Lux grasps it tightly. Edward takes her other hand.

"Okay! Everybody ready?"

I feel the boat tip over the edge. We start to fall forward.

I slam the stereopticon up to my eyes, squint through the foggy lens, and shout as loudly as I can . . .

"*The British Museum—the night of the Ophir exhibit!*"

THE NEW WORLD EXPLORERS

hooooomph!

I land on something hard and cold. I try to sit up, but a splitting pain rockets through my head and stops me. I lie back down and open my eyes. Lux is kneeling next to me.

"You okay?" she whispers.

With extra effort, I finally manage to sit up and look around. We're in a dark room with a thick velvet curtain in front of us. A crack of light seeps in through the bottom. I crawl over to the curtain and pull it back an inch.

"We're in the museum?" I whisper. "It worked?"

"It worked!" she says. "You're . . . brilliant!"

She throws her arms around me and kisses my cheek, which turns a brilliant beet red.

There's a rustle in the corner of the room. Edward slowly sits up and rubs the back of his head. "Where are we?" he asks.

"We're home!" Lux says.

"Everyone must be so worried looking for us," Edward says with a slight frown of concern. "We've been gone for days!"

We jump up and rush toward the heavy curtain. On my way, I see the stereopticon lying on the floor. I scoop it up.

When we burst through the curtain, we're shocked to find ourselves in the middle of the Ophir reception. Herds of people mingle about at the cocktail party. I recognize the old man who still has some mint sauce on his shoe from when I'd kicked my lamb chop at him.

"What? It's still going on?" asks Lux. She eyes a clock on the wall. "I remember looking at a clock before we entered the secret room. If everything is correct, we've been gone for only . . . six minutes?"

Edward looks irritated. "We have to find my grandfather at once!"

"They must still be sequestered," Lux says.

"Follow me! I know where they are!" he shouts.

Edward races off, with us trying to follow him through the crowd. He takes us down a strange elevator that looks as if it were built a hundred years ago. When the elevator opens, we come face-to-face with guards standing before the door to a chamber where the Alliance is meeting.

"Please—you have to let us in!" Edward begs. "We need to speak to my grandfather. It's an emergency!"

The guards glance at us skeptically, eyeing our tattered, dirty clothes and unkempt appearance.

"You don't understand—I'm Edward Weatherhead," Edward continues. "And this is Lux Lopez, Lorenzo Lopez's daughter."

CHAPTER THIRTEEN

"And I'm AZ," I chime in. I reach into my backpack and pull out the Alliance ring. "I'm Sir Arthur's nephew."

When they see Uncle Arthur's ring, they spring into action. One of them leads us to Lord Weatherhead's office, while the other goes to notify the Alliance.

We're sitting in large wingback chairs when the door opens and Lord Weatherhead and Uncle Arthur come in. They try to hide their reaction to our ragged appearance, but we can tell they're shocked and confused.

Lord Weatherhead slowly makes his way to the burgundy leather chair behind the desk. Uncle Arthur stands next to him, his hands clasped behind his back.

"What has happened?" Lord Weatherhead asks, no longer trying to hide his concern. "Tell us everything, from beginning to end, leaving no detail out."

And so we do. We tell him everything—or at least everything we can remember in the heat of the moment. I'm sure there are parts we're missing. The story spills out as we tumble over one another's words. It all comes gushing out like a raging waterfall. The more we say, the darker Lord Weatherhead's expression becomes.

When we're finished, Lord Weatherhead and Uncle Arthur exchange brief nods.

"Will you excuse us?" Lord Weatherhead asks. "Sir Arthur and I must confer privately." They slip through a door.

The room is silent as Edward, Lux, and I look at each other. All we can hear is the ticking clock.

Lord Weatherhead and Uncle Arthur return a few minutes later, though it feels like hours. They resume their same positions. They both have grave expressions.

"Only a few of us have even seen Ophir," Lord Weatherhead continues. "You, however, are the only ones to have ever entered the inner sanctum. Now tell me again: You gave Heinrich the Ruby Tablet? We need to know exactly how long he's had it, so we can calculate the damage. We must move quickly, children."

I sit up. "No. Wait. We forgot—Heinrich doesn't have the Ruby Tablet."

"He *doesn't*?"

"He doesn't," Edward confirms.

Lord Weatherhead and Uncle Arthur look confused.

I can't help but laugh a little, realizing we left out that part of the story. I look at Edward, who's trying to suppress a laugh too.

"We'd never give him the real Ruby Tablet, would we?" I ask.

"Never." Edward smiles.

"But if you didn't give Heinrich the *real* Ruby Tablet," Lord Weatherhead asks, "then what did you give him?"

"A lollipop," I say.

"Pardon?" One of Lord Weatherhead's big bushy eyebrows crawls up his forehead like a hairy white caterpillar. "A lollipop?" he repeats.

Now Lux is giggling. "Oh yeah—wait until you hear *this* part! It's the best!" She looks at Lord Weatherhead and Uncle Arthur as if prepping them for the world's greatest story.

I nod. "We made a fake Ruby Tablet using my lollipop recipe. I already had red food coloring in my backpack, and I also had the sugar and corn syrup I'd taken from the crates of German supplies."

Uncle Arthur stops us. "You did all this inside the inner sanctum?"

"Yep. The heat source was a little tricky. Remember, Edward?"

"A nightmare," Edward says. "But we rigged sheets of

copper over four evenly spaced fires we built on the floor. Then, of course, there was the mold."

"Another nightmare!" I grin. "We used the original tablet and made a reverse mold out of dirt we had dug up and mixed with water. Then we took the lollipop mixture, poured it into the mold, and let it set. When it was all done, we had ourselves a big red Ruby Tablet–shaped lollipop!"

Edward nods seriously. "Big," he repeats. "You've never seen a lollipop that big before."

"It may even have been the world's largest lollipop. I don't remember the dimensions."

"Oh, I do," Edward says. "It was sixty centimeters by

ninety centimeters—or roughly two feet by three feet," he adds with a helpful smile.

"I couldn't have done it without Edward," I tell Lord Weatherhead. "He saved the day with all the chemical mixing and science stuff. Plus, he did the lion's share of carving the hieroglyphs. I did some, with Edward's instruction, but he did most. That took a ton of time. All those little symbols—and we had to make them look real enough to fool Heinrich. We were practically official inner sanctum scribes by dawn."

"Of course, we had to change a *few* hieroglyphs to change the recipe," Edward inserts. "Just to be safe."

"Yeah," Lux chimes in. "You didn't want to go to all that trouble, only to find out the recipe works on a lollipop just as well as it works on the real Ruby Tablet!"

She smiles. I smile. Edward smiles too.

Lord Weatherhead just stares at us from behind his desk.

"And the real Ruby Tablet . . . ?" Uncle Arthur asks.

"Right where it belongs, in the inner sanctum," I say.

"And Heinrich?" he asks.

Suddenly, Edward, Lux, and I look at each other, our smiles fading.

"We have no idea where he is," I say, shaking my head. It leaves an uneasy feeling in my stomach—and not because of the gross-off foods still squirming around in there.

Lord Weatherhead sits back. "All right, then. Anything else you 'forgot'?"

"Oh yeah. One more thing." I reach in my pocket. "I found this."

I slide the gold ankh across the mahogany desk to Lord Weatherhead, who studies it carefully. Uncle Arthur bends down to peer at it as well.

"See?" I tell them excitedly. "It's proof that Ophir and

Meroë are the same city!"

"Yes, it is proof positive," Lord Weatherhead says. He slides the ankh back across the desk to me. "With this artifact, you can definitively link the city of Ophir with the city of Meroë." He pauses to throw a side glance at Uncle Arthur. "The question is, what do you want to *do* with that proof?"

"We want to show everyone where Ophir really is!" I say quickly.

"And we want everyone to know Heinrich is a big fat liar!" Edward adds.

"And we want the world to know we found Ophir!" Lux says.

Lord Weatherhead nods. "Ophir is a city filled with many secrets," he says. "Powerful secrets, such as the Ruby Tablet. Power can be used for good or evil. It can protect people or drive them to do terrible things."

"Now," Uncle Arthur chimes in, "the Alliance code states that when an explorer makes a discovery, that explorer can decide whether or not to reveal it to the world at large. Keep in mind that the Alliance does not exist to *suppress* facts or discoveries. Rather, we are dedicated to *protecting* any discoveries that could cause harm or be harmed themselves."

Lord Weatherhead smiles kindly at us. "You have the power to keep the Lost City of Secrets hidden, or you can show it to the world. The decision is yours—but you must make it now."

He hands the ankh to me, then settles back in his leather chair. Uncle Arthur straightens up and places his hands behind his back. Together, they stare at us. We can hear the clock ticking again.

They're waiting for an answer.

"So, guys?" Lux says. "What should we do?"

We three look at each other. It's a long, hard look. No

words are needed.

"Would you like some time to discuss it privately, perhaps?" Lord Weatherhead offers.

"No." I shake my head. "I think our decision is already made."

Edward and Lux nod.

I take a deep breath. "Even though it would be super cool to get credit for discovering the greatest archaeological find on earth, maybe the Ruby Tablet has too much power."

"People would fight for it," Lux adds. "Or even go to war."

"Perhaps it's better off staying precisely where it is," Edward says.

"A true archaeologist cares more about protecting treasures than about finding them," I say, quoting my mom. "Some things are safest when they're still lost. So, our decision is that the Lost City of Secrets should stay a secret."

I hand the gold ankh back to Lord Weatherhead once again.

He takes it, smiling.

Uncle Arthur nods at Lord Weatherhead. "And now, there's one more piece of business to take care of."

"Just some paperwork," Lord Weatherhead adds, his mouth twitching. "Please follow me."

We follow him to a subterranean level of the museum. It's located somewhere way, way beneath the basement.

"Only Alliance members are allowed on this level," Lord Weatherhead says.

Edward, Lux, and I share smiles.

When the elevator doors open, we pass several heavily armed guards and then find ourselves outside a set of wooden doors.

"Please wait here," Lord Weatherhead tells us, gesturing to a bench. He and Uncle Arthur proceed through the doors.

CHAPTER THIRTEEN

We sit there on the hard bench, shifting uncomfortably. I glance nervously at the armed guards.

"This must be *really* important paperwork," I whisper.

Finally, a uniformed guard comes out and escorts us through the doors. We're stunned when we step into a huge auditorium. A large AWE seal hangs above the brightly lit stage. The hushed room is filled with Alliance members sitting behind a long line of desks arranged in a U formation.

Lux sees her dad and gives him an excited wave. He winks at her, his face filled with pride.

Still shocked, we walk down a green carpeted aisle that reminds me a little of the Royal Road. We're directed to sit onstage. We squint into the lights and can barely see.

Lord Weatherhead takes the podium. "Ladies and gentlemen of the Alliance," he begins, "please allow me to introduce Lux, Edward, and AZ." He sweeps his hand toward us.

I gulp.

"From this day forward, by unanimous vote, they are officially lifelong members of the Alliance of World Explorers!"

The auditorium suddenly explodes with thunderous applause.

I can't believe what I'm hearing! Edward, Lux, and I all look at each other, shocked and amazed. We are officially members of the Alliance of World Explorers!

Lord Weatherhead presents us with our own gold Alliance rings. "In the face of extraordinary circumstances, you yourselves were extraordinary," he says.

I like the sound of that.

Uncle Arthur comes over and extends his arm for a handshake. But first, I reach into my bag to return his ring. He places his ring on his pinkie and nods. Now we shake hands, each of us wearing our own ring.

"Did you really eat jellied elephant mucus?" he asks me, still gripping my hand.

"Yep," I confirm. "As Heinrich said, it was a wonderful palate cleanser."

"Well done," Uncle Arthur says, looking impressed and giving my hand an extra squeeze.

* * *

That night, Uncle Arthur says it's finally time to go home. I stand in front of the museum, not sure how to say good-bye to Edward and Lux.

Lux surprises everybody with gifts. She gives her Tecpatl knife to Edward, who looks stunned and thanks her profusely. Then she gives me an Egyptian encyclopedia. I can't believe it either.

"I'll memorize every word," I tell her. "Wait and see."

She smiles. It's the best thing in the world. My cheeks turn pink, but I don't care.

Then Singh pulls up in the car, and Uncle Arthur and I get in. I wave at Edward and Lux through the window until they are specks.

At the airport, the *Invictrix* is waiting for us. After takeoff, Uncle Arthur leans back in his seat and studies me for a moment.

"I'll tell you a secret," he says. "Some people believe that when a person pledges to protect Ophir, they get a gift for keeping the secret."

"A gift?" I look at him. "What kind of gift?"

"You never know. It's from the ancients, and it's just between you and them. Could be bravery, wisdom—once I got more hair! But you'll know your gift when you see it."

I nod, though my mind races. A gift! I can hardly wait to discover what it is.

CHAPTER THIRTEEN

Just then, Uncle Arthur's satellite phone rings. Uncle Arthur answers, then hands me the phone.

"It's your parents 'checking up' on you," he says, rolling his eyes as he quotes them.

I freeze. What in the world will I say to them? Uncle Arthur gives me a knowing look and puts his finger to his lips. I nod back.

"How're you doing?" my mom asks when I come on the phone.

"Um . . . pretty good."

"Are you having fun? Are you behaving?"

"Um, yeah . . . I guess so."

"Where are you?" she asks. "Are you with Uncle Arthur?"

I look around the high-tech luxury jet. "Um . . ."

"Hang on, honey—your father wants to say hello."

My dad gets on the phone. "AZ?"

"Hey, Dad!"

"Hey, champ! Are you having a good time with your uncle? Better than expected?"

"Uh, well, you could say that."

"Don't let Arthur run you ragged," he says. "If he tries to get you to clean out his gutters, you just tell him you're afraid of heights."

"Oh, OK . . ."

Dad pauses for a second. "Son, I just want to tell you that your mom and I have been talking. We think . . . well, what I mean is . . . Well, we realize that digging up a woolly mammoth is a pretty amazing opportunity. We want you to fly out and join us so we can all experience this together. The only thing we ask is that you *promise* to get your grades up next year. Okay?"

I sit there holding the phone.

"Son?" The line crackles. "Can you hear me?"

"I hear you, Dad. But you know something? You and Mom

were right about computers and tech. They're fine and good, but real explorers need to know how to make calculations and solve complex problems on their own. So I was wondering, can you help me with my math when we get home? Also, I want to learn how to read hieroglyphs. OK, Dad?"

There's no response.

"Dad?"

It's my dad's turn to be speechless.

In the silence, I hear a buzz from the phone. Uncle Arthur takes it right from my hands.

"That's my call waiting," he says flatly into the phone. "Ta-ta."

Just like that, he hangs up on my dad and takes the incoming call.

I spin my gold octagonal Alliance ring around my finger while Uncle Arthur listens intently to whoever is on the other line. He barely speaks, saying only, "I see."

Uncle Arthur gets off the phone and sighs. "Well, there's good news and bad news," he says. "The bad news is, they failed to capture Heinrich. He's still on the loose. The good news is, he didn't get anything out of the inner sanctum. Not according to the sphinx."

I wrinkle my brow. "But I thought the sphinx was gone."

"The one you met is. She got to retire."

"Retire? I thought she *died*."

He shakes his head. "Sphinxes never die. They retire. Your sphinx is enjoying a time-share in Florida now. Anyway, the new sphinx who replaced her reports that the inner sanctum is safe. The city of Ophir has been resealed. Also, we got the chemical report back on that Ophirian ankh you found. The lab report indicates it may be made of orichalcum."

"Ori-what?"

"Oh-rih-CAL-cum," he repeats. "Orichalcum is the gold

produced in Atlantis."

I look up, stunned. "Atlantis? As in, massive-empire-lost-under-the-sea Atlantis?"

"That's the one." He smiles. "Is the world's grossest explorer ready for another adventure?"

I grin at Odd Uncle Arthur. "Ready and waiting, Sir Arthur! *Semper exploro!*"

End-of-Adventure Notes

Last night the Alliance of World
Explorers officially invited us to join.
A.W.E. - all three of us!! Lux, Edward
and even me!

The Alliance held a special vote and the
decision was unanimous. Lord Weatherhead gave us our own gold Alliance rings.
He said, "In the face of extaordinary
circumstances, you yourselves
were extraordinary."

I like the sound of that.

Semper Exploro!
-AZ

TOP SECRET!!!

WARNING:

THE FOLLOWING
INFORMATION IS
CLASSIFIED.

ONLY
EXPLORERS
MAY CONTINUE.

Explorers, Start Exploring!

Make Your Own Explorer's Kit

Use anything you want to hold all your tools:
a bag, a backpack, a lunch box, or even a dirty old pair of cargo shorts! In your kit, you should have the following items:

PEN

TAPE
(for taping stuff into your notebook)

NOTEBOOK

FLASHLIGHT
(plus backup batteries)

SIGNAL MIRROR

EMPTY JAR WITH LID
(for specimens)

BINOCULARS

MAGNIFYING GLASS

Create Your Own Adventure Journal

1) Get a notebook and a pencil or pen.

2) Title the first page:

MY ADVENTURE BOOK—
TOP SECRET!

3) Fill up your Adventure Journal!

★ List all the adventures you want to have!

★ Write down all the foods you want to try!

★ Record all the cool, weird, gross observations you make!

Use the following pages to get started!

My BIG Adventure List

All the ADVENTURES I want
to have Before I'm Grown-up!

WHAT?

WHERE?

WHY?

My BIG Adventure List

All the ADVENTURES I want
to have Before I'm Grown-up!

WHAT?

WHERE?

WHY?

My BIG Adventure List

All the ADVENTURES I want
to have Before I'm Grown-up!

WHAT?

WHERE?

WHY?

My BIG Food List

All the FOOD I want
to eat Before I'm Grown-up!

WHAT?

WHERE?

WHY?

My BIG Food List

All the FOOD I want
to eat Before I'm Grown-up!

WHAT?

WHERE?

WHY?

My BIG Food List

All the FOOD I want to eat Before I'm Grown-up!

WHAT?

WHERE?

WHY?

Explorer Observations

Write down all the things you see around you.
Use your senses (sight, sound, smell, taste,
and touch) to notice details!

Time and Date: _____

Location: _____

Observations: _____

_____

_____

Time and Date: _____

Location: _____

Observations: _____

_____

_____

_____

Time and Date: _____

Location: _____

Observations: _____

_____

_____

Make Your Own Papyrus Treasure Map

You can make
your own papyrus scroll,
just as the ancient Egyptians
did. You can then use the scroll
to create your own treasure map!

Have your friends use the map
to find a hidden treasure, or
keep your map to yourself so
only you can find your loot!

Here's how to make a
papyrus scroll:

1. Cover your work area with newspaper and lay an old kitchen towel over the top. (Ask an adult about which towel is a good one to use.)

2. In a shallow bowl, add equal amounts of white school glue and water. Mix until smooth.

3. Tear a large brown paper bag into two-inch-wide strips.

4. One at a time, dip each strip into the glue mixture and lay it on the towel. Make sure all the strips overlap slightly to form your scroll.

5. Once all the strips are placed, smooth them with your hands, pressing lightly.

6. Repeat this process with a second layer of strips. When done, smooth the scroll with your hands again.

7. Let the paper air-dry completely.

8. Decorate the papyrus scroll with markers. Write your name in hieroglyphs or draw a treasure map for a treasure hunt with your friends. Have fun!

Ruby Tablet Lollipops

Makes 12 Lollipops

YOU WILL NEED:

Twelve 4-inch lollipop sticks and a candy thermometer

1 cup granulated sugar

½ cup water

2 tablespoons light corn syrup

6 drops red food coloring

1 teaspoon cinnamon oil

Ask an adult to help you with this project.

1) Line a large rimmed baking sheet with parchment paper or aluminum foil. Arrange the lollipop sticks on the baking sheet, about 4 inches apart.

2) In a small heavy-duty saucepan, add the sugar, water, and corn syrup.

3) Bring to a boil over medium heat, whisking, until the sugar has dissolved.

4) Cover and boil the syrup for 1 minute.

5) Uncover and increase the heat to medium-high. Continue to cook the syrup, without stirring, until it reaches 300° F on a candy thermometer, 5–7 minutes.

6) Remove from heat and let cool for 5 minutes.

7) Stir in the food coloring and cinnamon oil.

8) Carefully spoon the syrup into 3-inch puddles over the top half of each lollipop stick.

9) Let cool completely and enjoy!

Master Blaster Exploding Foam

Ask an adult to help you with this project.

YOU WILL NEED:

A safe workspace

Safety goggles

Gloves

A funnel

¾ cup industrial-strength 30% hydrogen peroxide

Squirt of dish soap

An empty liter-sized soda bottle

Food coloring (optional)

A plastic cup

1 tablespoon active dry yeast

3 tablespoons water

Put on your safety goggles and gloves. Using a funnel, pour the hydrogen peroxide into the empty soda bottle. Add the dish soap and food coloring, if using.

In the plastic cup, mix the active dry yeast with the water. With a parent or guardian nearby, use the funnel to carefully pour the yeast-and-water mixture into the soda bottle.
Then . . .

STAND BACK!

Really True and Really Gross Facts about Ancient Egypt

Ophir is a real lost city! It's mentioned in the Bible, but no one today knows its location or whether it actually existed. Go to www.AZWorldExplorer.com to learn more!

Pharaohs never let the public see their hair. From childhood on, each pharaoh wore a heavy crown, or *nemes*, that was a blue-and-white headdress (like King Tut's This resulted in some seriously deformed heads!

In the 1300s, people ground mummies into powder and ingested them as a cure for illnesses.

King Pepi II of Egypt didn't want flies to land on him, so he always surrounded himself with several naked slaves whose bodies were smeared with honey to attract insects.

Since they didn't have antibiotics, ancient Egyptians put moldy bread on infected wounds. This isn't as odd as it seems, though. Penicillin, an antibiotic used widely today to treat infections, is derived from a fungus.

King Charles II of England would collect the dust that fell off mummies. He used it on his skin, believing the "greatness" would rub off.

To keep away lice and other insects, ancient Egyptians supposedly shaved most of the hair off their bodies.

Ancient Egyptian embalmers would sometimes suck a mummy's brain out through a straw that went up the nose. Then the intestines were put inside stone vessels called canopic jars. In fact, nearly every organ was placed in its own jar. The only internal organ that was not removed was the heart. Egyptians considered it to be the "seat of the soul."

Ancient Egyptian Gods

Amun (creator god) and **Ra** (sun god) were eventually combined into the chief god **Amun-Ra**.

Anubis is the god of mummification and the dead.

Aten is the visible disk of the sun, worshiped during the reign of Pharaoh Akhenaten.

Atum is god of the setting sun.

Bastet is the cat-headed goddess.

Geb is the earth god.

Hapi is the Nile god.

Hathor is the love goddess, sometimes represented as a cow.

Horus is two gods—**Horus the Younger** and **Horus the Elder**—later combined into one god.

Isis is the goddess of healing and feminine fertility.

Khnum is the ram-headed god, who created human beings.

Maat is the goddess of truth and justice.

Min is the god of masculine fertility.

Montu is the war god.

Nut is the sky goddess.

Osiris is the god of the underworld.

Ptah is the father of the gods.

Seth is the envious god of disorder.

Shu is the goddess of air and wind.

Sobek is the crocodile god.

Tefnut is the lion-headed goddess.

Thoth is the god of the moon and scribe of the gods.

WANT TO KEEP EXPLORING?

Go to
www.AZWorldExplorer.com

for more about the

ALLIANCE OF WORLD EXPLORERS!

Get an official **AWE** Identification Badge.

Meet real world **EXPLORERS.**

Find out how to get an Official World Explorer Kit.

Get recipes for the **GROSSEST** meals in the world.

Find out how to do an archaeological dig in your backyard.

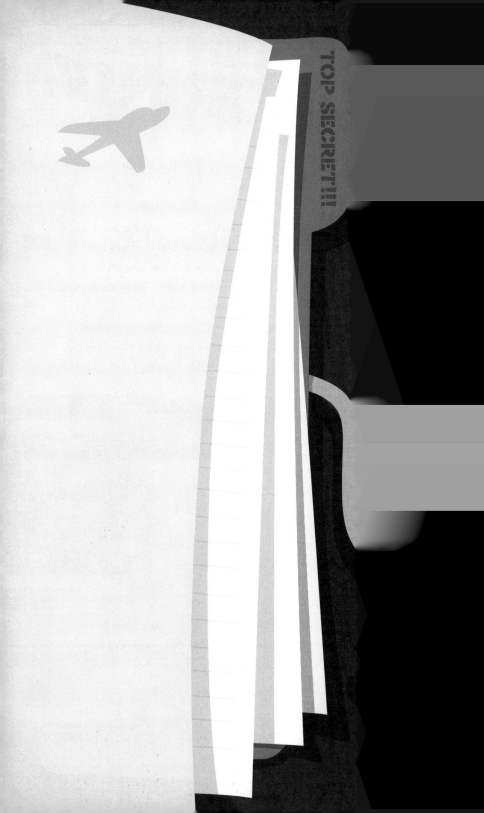

About the Authors

Steve Henke

Andrew Zimmern

is a world-renowned chef, writer, teacher, and television personality. He has won four prestigious James Beard Awards for Outstanding Television Food Personality and for his hit show, *Bizarre Foods*, on the Travel Channel. When not in airplanes, buses, or hovercraft transport stations, he lives in Minneapolis, MN, with his family.

H. E. McElhatton

is the author of *Pretty Little Mistakes*, *Million Little Mistakes*, and *Jennifer Johnson Is Sick of Being Single*. She's a PEN/ Faulkner nominee and a commentator for Minnesota Public Radio. Her stories have been heard on *This American Life*, the BBC, and *All Things Considered*. She lives in Castle Danger, MN, with her pug, Walter.